Shelby's Best Friend

SHELBY SHAYNE STORIES

2

VeraLee Wiggins

Pacific Press Publishing Association
Boise, Idaho
Oshawa, Ontario, Canada

Dedication:

This one's for you, Lisa.
My sweet, precious love.
Now and always.

Edited by Marvin Moore
Designed by Dennis Ferree
Cover and inside art by Stephanie Britt
Typeset in 13/15 Weiss

Copyright © 1994 by
Pacific Press Publishing Association
Printed in the United States of America
All Rights Reserved

Library of Congress Cataloging-in-Publication Data:
Wiggins, VeraLee, 1928-
    Shelby's best friend / VeraLee Wiggins.
        p.   cm. — (The Shelby Shayne series ; bk. 2.)
    Sequel to: Shelby's big prayer.
    Sequel: Shelby's big scare.
    Summary: Shelby needs God's help as she tries to take care of her
new puppy, make friends with a black classmate, and deal with an
obnoxious boy at school as well as with the troubled girl across the
street.
    ISBN 0-8163-1189-7
    [1. Christian life. 2. Dogs. 3. Schools. 4. Aunts. 5. Uncles.] I. Title.
II. Series: Wiggins, VeraLee, 1928-   Shelby Shayne series ; bk. 2.
PZ7.W6386Sc   1994
[Fic]—dc20   93-27279
                                                            CIP
                                                             AC

94 95 96 97 98 ● 5 4 3 2 1

Contents

CHAPTER

1

Princess Ebony

Shelby Shayne had a dog of her very own! An eensy, teensy black Pomeranian named Princess Ebony. She'd just brought the puppy home today. The tiny black ball of fluff sleeping in her arms stirred as she gazed lovingly at it. Even seeing it, she almost couldn't believe it. Her own dog! "Thank You, God," she whispered for the millionth time.

Bedtime was approaching. Shelby yawned and started down the hall toward her bedroom, carrying Princess Ebony. Suddenly she stopped, wondering where her "baby" was going to sleep. She'd talked about letting it sleep with her, but she wasn't sure. She retraced her steps to the living room.

"Auntie," she said, dropping to the couch beside Aunt Rachel, "do you think my puppy could sleep with me?"

Aunt Rachel held out her arms for the one-pound baby. "Of course, she can sleep with you," she said, stroking the tiny body. She cuddled the tiny creature for a moment, then got up and handed it back to Shelby. "Maybe we should put a towel over the sheet, just in case." She smiled up at Shelby as they hurried down the hall. Although Shelby was only eleven years old, she towered over her aunt by several inches.

Shelby found an extra-large towel on the bathroom shelf, folded it in thirds, and arranged it on the bed. Climbing in beside it, she carefully placed the puppy on it. The puppy curled up on the towel totally content.

"You won't roll on her, will you?" Auntie asked.

"I hope not. That would kill her." Shelby peered up at her aunt, who stood beside the bed. "Do you think I will?"

"No. You're a quiet sleeper, and you awaken easily. Just remember the puppy while you sleep. And if she wakes up, you'd better take her to the papers we put in the bathroom." Auntie leaned down and kissed Shelby on the cheek. "Have a good night. If you need me, just call."

"I guess you aren't sleeping with me tonight?"

Aunt Rachel shook her dark head. "I'm afraid it'll be sort of crowded if I try to get in there too." Then she smiled. "But if you need me, be sure to call. We'll think of something." She kissed Shelby's cheek again and quietly left the room.

Shelby had been living with her aunt and uncle in their beautiful new home in Veneta, Oregon. She'd been with them about four months—ever since Mom had died. Shelby'd had some bad nightmares, so

Auntie had slept with her a lot.

Shelby pulled the puppy close. She could hardly believe she had a puppy of her very own. She'd prayed so hard—and this tiny baby was God's answer.

After Mom died, wanting a puppy had become an obsession. She'd thought of nothing else and prayed for a dog constantly. Then God had performed what seemed to Shelby like a miracle, finding this puppy for her. It *had* to be the cutest and sweetest dog in all the world!

"Thank You, Father," she whispered as she snapped off the light. She'd just thanked Him a half-hour ago during family worship. She must have said "Thank You" a million times already, and still it didn't seem enough. She fell asleep in a happy glow.

Suddenly Shelby awakened. Wondering what had awakened her, she felt something at her side. The puppy stirred and struggled to its feet. Grabbing her light robe and the dog, she rushed to the bathroom. She carefully put the puppy on the newspapers on the floor. "Potty," she said softly. She repeated the word about a dozen times, and the puppy made a tiny little puddle on the paper. Shelby could hardly believe it! She almost had her baby potty-trained already. Telling the tiny animal what a good girl she was, Shelby wadded up the paper and spread another.

After washing her hands, she carried the puppy back to bed. Then she crawled in beside it. The puppy rolled to its round little back and began chewing on Shelby's fingers. The tiny animal chewed so gently that Shelby fell asleep while it played.

The dog awakened Shelby three more times during

the night, and each time it did its "thing" on the paper.

"She didn't mess up her towel even once," Shelby reported in the morning. "But I feel sort of tired."

"Did she cry much?" Uncle James asked.

Shelby had forgotten all about that possibility. She shook her dark blond head. "She didn't cry once. Just wiggled until I took her to the bathroom. When I brought her back, she always snuggled down and fell asleep again."

"Well, come and eat breakfast," Aunt Rachel said. "It's almost time for you to go to school."

Shelby sat down to a steaming bowl of oat bran with brown sugar and milk. As soon as Uncle James asked the blessing, she dug into the cereal. Then a thought popped into her mind. "Who's going to take care of Princess Ebony while I'm gone?" she asked.

Auntie smiled and held up her left hand, toast and all. "I guess I'm elected," she said. "I'll just make her a bed in a nice box and put it beside my desk. She can sleep there until you come home." She reached over and patted Shelby's arm. "Don't worry, kiddo, I'll feed her lunch. And, yes, I'll be sure to give her exactly as much Science Diet Puppy Food as Emil said. We want her to grow healthy and strong." Emil was the man they'd bought the puppy from.

Having no other choice, Shelby got herself ready and ran out to the road. She'd walk to the end of Marina Drive to catch the bus on Ellmaker Road.

"Wait, Shayne. Wait up." Shelby stopped when she heard Molly's voice. Molly, just a few months younger than Shelby, lived across the road. Shelby stood about six inches taller, and Molly looked about the same number of inches wider. Her blond hair was much lighter than Shelby's. And every time Molly made the s sound, she lisped. When she said "Shayne," it sounded like "Thayne."

Molly soon walked in stride with Shelby, puffing hard. "How come you didn't wait?" she scolded. "I bet all you can think about is that dog of yours."

Shelby nodded happily. "Just about. Oh, Molly, it didn't even wet the bed once. Isn't that cool?"

Molly's feet kept hurrying toward the bus stop. Shelby thought she wouldn't answer. "I should hope so," she finally lisped. "If you're going to sleep with a dog that wets the bed, I'm never touching you again. And that's the truth."

The bus pulled up ahead of them, and they took off running. As Shelby hurried to the back of the bus, her eyes met those of a red-headed boy. "Hi, Shayne," he said.

"Hi, yourself, Shane," Shelby answered with a friendly smile. She'd met Shane Anderson at the lake near her aunt and uncle's house during the summer. Sharing a name had probably caused them to become friends. Never mind that it was his first name and her last. Anyway, he was a nice guy. And though he looked more like he should be in fifth grade, he was an eighth-grader.

"How's the dog?" Shane asked. He'd come over to see the puppy last night, but Molly had gotten there first and wouldn't let him hold it. "Did it make you crazy, crying for its mother?"

Shelby reached her seat, sat down, and scooted over to give Molly room. "It didn't cry at all," she called back as the bus started moving.

Fifteen minutes later the bus pulled up in front of the school and stopped. When Shelby jumped down from the bus, LeeAnne, her only other friend, grabbed her hand. "How's that darling puppy?" the pretty black girl asked as they walked toward the school. LeeAnne's mother had brought her to see the puppy last night too, but Molly wouldn't let her hold it either.

"She's great, LeeAnne. I slept with her and didn't even roll over on her."

Molly nudged between Shelby and LeeAnne. "I wish you two could think about something besides dogs," she grumbled. "I suppose that's all we'll ever talk about for the rest of our lives." (With her lisp all the *s*'s came out like *th*'s; "*suppose*" turned into "*thuppothe*.")

Fortunately, Molly's bad mood didn't spoil LeeAnne's enthusiasm over Shelby's new puppy. Classes soon began, and Shelby tried to turn her mind to math. But try as she might, she couldn't get her brand-new puppy out of her mind. She barely heard the teacher talking and missed most of the instructions.

She thought the day would *never* pass. Maybe the puppy would cry for her. What if Auntie forgot to feed it? Auntie might get upset if the dog kept her from her work. No, she wouldn't. Auntie didn't get upset easily.

Finally, after "two hundred years," Shelby hurried to the band room, feeling happy. She loved to play her flute in band. And today she felt especially glad that band was the last period of the day. She'd soon be home with her puppy, Princess Ebony.

But when she stepped into the band room, Jonathan Greenflower started yelling. "Well, if it isn't Little

Orphan Annie! Hey, everyone, take a good look at her big, blank eyes!" Jon had picked on Shelby ever since the first day of school, when she'd been forced into telling the class her mother had died.

Shelby felt like turning around and running back the way she'd come, but she didn't. She held her chin a little higher and marched to her seat in the flute section.

"What did you do to your hair, Orphan Annie?" Jon yelled. "I thought it was red and curly."

Shelby's insides churned so badly she thought she might throw up, but she tried her best not to let it show. She casually opened her case, pulled out her flute, and started warming up. As she played some scales, she felt a little calmer and silently thanked her cousin Sandy. Shelby hadn't played before she came to live with her aunt and uncle. Auntie and Uncle bought the flute, and Sandy taught her a whole year's music lessons during the summer. In September Sandy went away to Milo Adventist Academy, a boarding school. Shelby missed her older cousin a lot, but thanks to her, Shelby could play as well as any of the kids.

She tried to tune out Jon's rude laugh and remarks as she listened to her flute's clear, bell-like tones.

"Jonathan Greenflower, why don't you just stick your trumpet down that big, ugly mouth of yours!" LeeAnne screamed, stopping Shelby's scale in the middle. A bunch of the kids started clapping for LeeAnne, but just then, Mrs. Beecher rushed in and wrecked it. Upset as she felt, Shelby noticed how tall and pretty Mrs. Beecher looked in her dark pants and silky gray shirt. Shelby knew *she* was going to be tall too. If she could end up like Mrs. Beecher, she wouldn't mind at all.

"What's going on?" the teacher asked, distributing sheets of music. "Do I rate all this applause?" No one said a word. Mrs. Beecher raised her arms, and band practice began.

An hour and fifteen minutes later Molly and Shelby jumped off the bus, and Shelby took off running. She simply couldn't wait another minute to see her new dog. She'd temporarily forgotten Molly, but feet pounding hard on the road reminded her.

"Hey, where's the fire?" Molly yelled. "Wait for me, Shayne. You aren't even nice."

Shelby slowed. "Hurry, then, Molly. I can't wait to see Princess Ebony."

Molly's smile turned upside down. She walked fifty feet before breaking the silence. "I guess you don't want me to come over then," she said. (*Guess* sounded like *geth.*) "I was hoping we could ride down to the lake."

She got the first part right. Shelby didn't want anyone to come over.

CHAPTER

2

Molly or Princess Ebony?

Shelby had waited all day to play with her new baby, but she couldn't say that to Molly. Molly needed someone to make her feel loved. Her dad and stepmother sure didn't!

"You can come over, Molly," Shelby said, trying to sound sincere. "But I won't be able to go anywhere. I have a lot to do to care for Princess Ebony." They'd nearly reached their houses by this time.

Molly jerked her face away from Shelby. "I can take a hint," she said, stomping toward her house.

" 'Bye, Molly," Shelby called. Molly acted as if she hadn't heard. Shelby gave up and raced into her house.

"Auntie," she called, tearing into the house. "Where's my puppy?"

"Down here," Aunt Rachel called from her office at the end of the hall. "Come on in."

Shelby almost flew down the hall to the office where her aunt worked with her computer, doing typing for people. Now that Shelby was so near to seeing her puppy, the thought almost made her breathless. She stopped at the door and greeted Auntie. "Has she been a bother?" she asked.

Aunt Rachel shook her head and released the tiny puppy. Princess Ebony ran as fast as her little legs would go, straight to Shelby. She scooped the puppy into her arms and cuddled it close. A few happy tears ran from her eyes, but she wiped them away quickly. "Was she a big nuisance today?" she asked again.

"Not exactly," Aunt Rachel said with a smile. "She's so precious I can hardly keep my hands off her."

The puppy snuggled against Shelby. Shelby sighed. "Good," she said. "I hope she won't do anything to make you mad at her."

"Don't worry about that," Auntie said. "I'm hooked."

"Did she eat lunch?" Shelby asked.

Aunt Rachel laughed. "Yeah, she ate. When I sat in the bathroom."

Shelby didn't understand.

"She wouldn't eat unless I stayed with her," Auntie explained. "Every time I left she cried; when I went back in, she gobbled food." She laughed. "And after she finished, I had to bring her down here and put her into this cardboard box. You have a sociable little friend there!"

Shelby carried her baby upstairs to the rocking chair. "Hush, little baby, don't say a word," she sang, rocking gently. "Mommy's going to buy you a mockingbird." She continued through all the verses, finishing with, "You'll still be the sweetest little baby in town." Her eyes filled with tears again as she looked at the teeny tiny ball of black fluff. Trust gleamed from the soft brown eyes. What was the matter with her, anyway? She hardly ever cried. "Oh, Ebony. Bonny, Bonny, I love you so much," she whispered. "I'll always take care of you and never let anything hurt you." The puppy's eyes never left hers. She loved the puppy so much she thought she couldn't contain it all.

The wee dog fell asleep in Shelby's arms, so she rocked it quietly, barely able to believe she had a dog—and especially this beautiful purebred Pomeranian. "Thank You, God," she whispered.

Hey! All this thinking reminded her that she needed to send in the American Kennel Club papers to register her puppy. Emil, the breeder, had given them to her and told her to send them in as soon as she chose a suitable name for her puppy.

"Shelby," Auntie called, coming from her office. "We need to send in your puppy's registration papers."

"I was just thinking the same thing," Shelby said. "I'll lay Ebony down, and we can get right to it." She put the puppy in the box Aunt Rachel had brought from the office, but Princess Ebony's brown eyes popped open, and she put her front feet up on the side of the box, crying.

"Wow, I think she wants me to hold her."

Auntie laughed. "You figured that right, kiddo."

Uncle James came home from work. He was an architect and worked in Eugene, a large city about twelve miles east. He walked in just in time to hear the puppy cry. "I believe she could be easily spoiled," he said with a silly grin.

Shelby wanted to snatch the crying puppy into her arms. But she wanted to please Uncle too. She'd better not spoil it. She looked through his glasses into his clear, bright blue eyes. "What should I do?" she asked.

"Pick it up," he said, laughing. "Don't you know babies need to be loved into security?"

Shelby had the puppy snuggled under her chin in two seconds.

Aunt Rachel laughed too. "OK, go get the papers, Shelby." She raised her dark eyebrows at Shelby. "We want this thing to be legally yours, don't we?"

"Yes," Shelby said eagerly. "Oh, yes! I'll get them." She dashed to her room, opened a shallow drawer, and pulled out the envelope. Then she hurried back to the living room. "Here's the stuff he gave me," she said, handing the blue envelope to Auntie.

Auntie took the papers, sat beside the dining-room table, and patted the chair next to her. "Come on, kiddo." Shelby sat down, and Auntie helped her fill out the forms telling the puppy's full name, sex, and color. Emil, the breeder, had filled in the breed of dog, birthdate, and parents' names.

"Let's take it to the post office," Shelby urged when they finished. "We'll get it back one day sooner, since our mailman's already gone."

"OK," Uncle James said, "I'll run you girls downtown. I need to deliver some papers to Harold's Market, anyway."

As the three burst out the door, they almost ran over

Molly. "We were just going to the post office," she said. "Come with us."

Molly climbed into the back seat with Shelby before she noticed the dog. "You're not taking that thing to the post office!" she yelled.

"Sure I am," Shelby said, laughing. "Why not?"

"Because [becauth] it's [ith] a dog."

Uncle pulled into the post-office parking lot, and Shelby jumped out. "Know what we're mailing?" she asked her short, plump friend as they walked toward the door.

"How would I know?"

Shelby's wide smile turned into a joyous laugh. "We're mailing Princess Ebony's official papers. Now she'll be legally mine."

Molly looked as if she were about to snap at Shelby, but another woman pushing envelopes through the slot noticed the puppy. "What is that?" she asked, pointing at the dog.

"It's a dog," Shelby said.

"Oh. But it's so tiny."

Shelby explained all about her new puppy.

As they hurried across the parking lot to the car, a teenage boy stopped Shelby. "Is that dog real?" he asked.

Just then, the puppy moved. "It's real," Shelby said.

"It's the cutest dog I've ever seen," the boy said. Shelby climbed into the car and sat down beside Molly.

Molly looked mad. Really mad. "I think it's perfectly disgusting," she said. She really said, "Ith perfectly dithguthting."

Auntie turned around toward the back seat. "What is?" she asked.

"The way Shelby gets people to make over her dumb dog."

No one answered. Shelby couldn't think of anything to say, so the car remained quiet all the way to Harold's Market and on home.

"Want to help me feed her?" Shelby asked when they got inside the house.

Molly hesitated. "Will you play with me when we're through?"

The only thing that sounded fun to Shelby was holding her puppy. "OK," she said, sounding half-hearted.

"You won't practice your flute or anything?"

"Not for a while. I'll have to later, though."

At last Molly smiled. "OK, let's get that food ready."

Shelby pulled a can from the refrigerator. Auntie had put a plastic lid on the food, then a zippered plastic bag around the can. Shelby smiled. She didn't have to worry about the stinky dog food contaminating their food. She put a small spoonful into the puppy's dish and carried it to the bathroom. Molly followed.

Princess Ebony almost dove into the food when Shelby put it on the floor. A moment later her back feet left the floor and dangled in the air.

"Hey, she's doing a handstand!" Molly yelled. The dog stopped eating and forced all four feet to the floor. She stuck her head into the food, and up went her back feet. This time the dog didn't stop eating but struggled to get her back feet on the floor while she stuffed her mouth. The girls laughed out loud.

"OK," Molly said five minutes later, "let's go play with our Barbies."

Shelby struggled to her feet. Ebony stopped eating and watched Shelby.

As the girls closed the bathroom door, they heard a tiny cry.

Shelby stopped. Molly grabbed her hand. "She's all right. Let's go play."

Shelby didn't move. "Molly," she said, "we can't go off and leave her locked in a bathroom crying!"

"You promised."

Shelby didn't answer but returned to the bathroom and dropped to the floor. "Oh, Bonny, Bunny, I can't let you cry." She held the elated puppy for a moment, then set her before her food again. Bonny Bunny Ebony dipped her head into the food, and her back feet flew off the floor again.

Molly laughed from the doorway. Shelby, who'd already forgotten Molly, felt relieved to hear her laugh. Molly soon remembered and choked off her laughter. "Come on, Shelby, and play. You promised."

Shelby gave her pup one last look and stepped through the door again. The crying began instantly. Shelby put her hand on the bathroom doorknob.

"If you open that door, I'm going home, and I'll never speak to you again!" Molly's face looked as though she meant every shouted word.

CHAPTER

3

Molly's Rude Stepmother

When Molly said she'd never speak to Shelby again, Shelby pictured herself alone, without friends, the way it was when she first came to Oregon. The thought terrified her. Molly wasn't the ideal best friend, but she was a whole lot better than no one.

But the puppy had no one besides her. Ebony had to come first. She opened the door and sat beside the baby while it ate. Soon the puppy decided it had had enough to eat. It waddled over to Shelby and climbed into her lap. "Hey," Shelby said, "we can take her with us." Lifting the dog gently into her arms, she followed Molly to her bedroom.

Shelby put the puppy on the bed. Opening a drawer,

she noticed a pair of pajamas for her Berry Baby, a baby doll about eleven inches tall. She held up the pink bit of flannel. "Look, Molly," she said. "Bunny can be our doll."

She zipped the tiny pajamas on the puppy, then changed to a little pink dress. Both girls laughed when she added the matching wide-brimmed hat. "I have to show Uncle and Auntie," Shelby said.

Uncle James and Aunt Rachel walked into the bedroom just then, and they laughed too. "She's darling," Auntie said. "When you hold her straight toward me so I can't see her nose, she looks exactly like a kitten. Be very careful not to hurt her little legs when you change her clothes."

The girls played with their new "doll" until it fell asleep. Shelby refused to bother the sleeping puppy, so Molly went home.

After dinner they were all sitting in the front room. "Have you been thinking about the big events coming up?" Uncle asked.

Shelby shook her head.

Aunt Rachel sat on Uncle's lap. "Come on, Shelby," she said. "You couldn't forget." Shelby shook her head again. Auntie slid onto the couch beside Shelby. "Do you remember anything special about the eighth of November?"

Shelby thought again. Then she did remember. "Sandy's coming home for the weekend. Hey, she can meet Bunny!"

"Bingo!" Uncle said. "And I don't suppose you remember why Sandy's coming home?"

It took a moment for Shelby to remember that

November 10 would be her twelfth birthday. She'd decided she wouldn't have any more birthdays with Mom gone. But somehow she didn't feel sad anymore. She turned happy eyes to meet Uncle's. "Yes! She's coming home for my birthday!"

Uncle laughed quietly. "I thought you'd never remember. Have you given any thought to what you'd like for your birthday?"

Shelby looked down into those precious brown eyes. "How could I ever want anything again, Uncle? I have it all right here in my arms. Oh, I can't wait for Sandy to meet Bunky."

"Bunky!" Aunt Rachel repeated. "Where did that name come from?"

Shelby giggled and shrugged. "I meant *Ebony—Bonny—Bunny*—and it came out *Bunky*." She giggled again. "She's too little for *Princess Ebony*. The name's bigger than she is."

Uncle nodded. "I can see that."

Shelby practiced her flute for an hour. A little later the family read a chapter from the Bible and prayed together. Then Shelby took her little black Ebony to bed. She thanked God one more time for giving her such a fantastic puppy, then told Him good night and closed her eyes.

She'd almost fallen asleep when a big, black-faced Siamese cat popped into her mind. She jumped from her bed, snatched up the sleeping puppy, and raced back to the living room. "I got so busy with Bunky tonight that I forgot the cats!" she said, puffing. "I'll get dressed and go take care of them." Shelby cat-sat for some neighbors who were in Arizona. She usually went there before coming home from school, but today she'd forgotten all about it.

"Don't get so excited, kiddo," Aunt Rachel said, motioning Shelby to sit down on the couch. "Is their food and water all gone every day?"

Shelby sat down. "No. They have lots of food and water."

"Go on back to bed, then. It won't hurt them to miss seeing you one day. You're more faithful than the Strattons could ever expect."

After a little more talking, Shelby went back to bed. She got paid two-and-a-half dollars every day for caring for the cats and petting them for an hour. The money added up fast, and Shelby didn't want to lose the job. She didn't want to neglect the cats, either.

The puppy got her up only twice that night, and Shelby awakened the next morning early, eager to meet the day. "I'm going to do the cats this morning," she told her uncle and aunt. "I'll feel better if I know they're all right."

Five minutes later Shelby hurried through the Strattons' living room and hall to the family room. The big Siamese she called King Tut burst through without a glance in her direction. That's how he always acted. Princess, the Persian, ran around and between her feet, mewing. That's how *she* always acted. Shelby refilled the food and water dishes, then scooped out the litter boxes. After washing her hands with soap and water, she played with Princess for half an hour, then put King Tut back in the family room and left.

When she and Molly climbed aboard the bus, Shane Anderson greeted Shelby. "How's the kitten—I mean puppy?" he asked. "When can I see it again? Will Molly let me hold it now?"

Shelby grinned. "Any time, Shane. I'd love to show you. And Molly doesn't even like her anymore."

"I do too," Molly insisted. "We dressed her in doll clothes last night."

"Well, come over any time," Shelby repeated.

Later during math class, when Shelby searched her notebook for her math paper, she couldn't find it. "I know I did it," she whispered to LeeAnne. She'd been faithful about her homework, so her teacher gave her another day to find it.

When band period came, she didn't rush to the music room. She hated going through that door because Jon Greenflower always had something mean to say about her being an orphan. Maybe today he wouldn't.

But he did. "Here's the poor little orphan," he bellowed. "Who bought your flute for you—the Salvation Army? Are you planning to play in their band?" Most of the boys laughed. Some of the girls did too. "Maybe we should take up a collection for the orphan," he added.

A titter of laughter barely started when LeeAnne stormed over to Jon. "Do you know what you are?" she shouted. "You're a big, yellow-bellied bully! Your name, Greenflower, says what you are. A little green flower."

"Way to go, LeeAnne," someone said. A wave of laughter began, but stopped suddenly when Jon started in on LeeAnne.

"You'd better stand up for the orphan," he yelled. "She's the only kid in school who can't find anyone to be with except a Sambo."

The kids gasped at his cruel words. Just then, Mrs.

Beecher came sailing in, all eager to start band. She didn't even notice the kids were extra quiet that day.

Before she went home that afternoon, Shelby took care of the cats again, even though she'd already cared for them that morning. As she brushed Princess, she thought about Jon Greenflower. How could anyone be so mean? And he looked so nice—tall, blond, and good looking.

She'd barely noticed LeeAnne's color. She was so lively and friendly, she just seemed like an extra-nice girl. Extra pretty too. Did the other kids mind LeeAnne being black? Not that Shelby could tell. But Jon was right about one thing. The girls hadn't swarmed all over LeeAnne to make friends.

Then she thought about the bad time Jon gave her. Why did he hit on that orphan stuff so hard? When he'd first started, Auntie and Uncle had offered to adopt Shelby. Maybe if they did, the trouble would be all over. Maybe if she could tell Jon that she really had parents, he'd shut up, and LeeAnne wouldn't have to yell at him anymore. Strange—LeeAnne had told her to ignore Jon, but when he picked on Shelby, LeeAnne couldn't keep her mouth shut.

Suddenly the hour she usually spent with the cats had passed and another half-hour too. She finished up and hurried home.

Auntie met her at the door with Princess Ebony in her arms. "Well," she said with a smile. "This little thing climbed out of every box I could find today. Then she lay at my feet under the desk, exhausted."

Shelby reached for the puppy. "Oh. We can't let her wet on the carpets."

Aunt Rachel nodded vigorously. "Right. And she insists on being right with us every second. Uncle suggested building a little playpen for her. Something we could carry around. What do you think?"

"Sounds good to me. If he wants to do it."

Aunt Rachel put a frozen casserole into the oven and went back to the office to finish a job.

Shelby put the puppy on a towel on the floor and held a piece of an old soft bathrobe belt in front of her. The dog jumped at the belt and snatched it in her teeth. Then she rolled onto her back and pawed at the belt with her front feet. "Oh, Bunny, Bunny," Shelby crooned, "you're the sweetest little dog in the whole world." Then with no warning, the puppy dropped to the towel and fell asleep.

Shelby decided to call Molly to see if she wanted to do their math together. But Aggie, Molly's stepmother, answered. "Molly's working," she snapped when Shelby asked for her friend. Then Aggie slammed the receiver in Shelby's ear.

CHAPTER

4

A Party for Bunky

Wow. That woman didn't even try to be nice. Shelby suddenly felt even sorrier for Molly and thankful for her own loving home.

She practiced her flute, then ate dinner with Auntie and Uncle. "Sandy will be home tomorrow afternoon," Uncle said as they cleared the table and loaded the dishwasher. "I'm sort of eager to see her."

"Me too!" Shelby echoed. "I can't wait to see how she likes Bunky." Oops, she'd done it again. Bunky.

"She'll like *Bunky*," Aunt Rachel said. "She'll probably want one just like Bunky." Her laughing eyes twinkled as she met Shelby's.

Shelby laughed out loud. "I'm sorry," she said. "I don't know where that word's coming from."

"Don't be sorry, kiddo. That little piece of fluff looks much more like a Bunky than a Princess Ebony."

"But her name's Princess Ebony. It's too late to change it. We've already sent it in."

"Who cares?" Uncle asked, peering at the stove burner he was scrubbing. "Lots of people have nicknames." He stopped and grinned at Shelby. "Even people more important than Bunky." Then he kept looking at Shelby with a strange look in his eyes.

"What's wrong, Uncle?" Shelby asked. "Do I have food on my face or something?"

He chuckled. "No. I just can't get over how much you look like your mother. She was my sister, you know. Sometimes it seems almost as if God has given her back to me in you, my sweet Shelby."

Shelby laughed quietly. Uncle looked so much like Mom that Shelby had thought the same about him. She thought about telling him but couldn't quite get the words out. She nodded. *Thank You, God,* she thought.

After they had the kitchen shining, Uncle snooped through the garage until he found an old plywood bookkeeping sign and several small boards. "These boards are the frame of your playpen," he told Shelby. "We also need some lightweight screen. Could you two get some while I put this together?"

Shelby grabbed Bunky and followed Auntie to the car. A few minutes later they hurried down the aisle in the Veneta Hardware store. Everyone they passed either asked about the tiny puppy or smiled at them. One girl about Shelby's age asked what it was. Then she said she'd never seen such a beautiful dog. She asked Shelby where she'd gotten Bunky. Shelby's heart swelled almost out of her chest.

Auntie soon found the screen, and a few minutes

later Shelby handed the package to Uncle. He'd put the frame together already. "Think you're strong enough to stretch the screen over the frame while I staple?" he asked Shelby. "It's a tough job."

She pulled hard while he stapled the screen all the way around. When they had finished, it looked nice. It was about four feet long, two feet wide, and a little more than knee high. "Wow!" Shelby said. "She'll like this, because she can watch us and see everything we do through the screen. I didn't know you were a carpenter, Uncle."

Uncle grinned all over his face. "Anyone could have made that, Shelby. Well, don't just stand there. Get some blankets and put Bunky in it. We have to see if she likes it."

Shelby put some soft rags in one end of the pen and newspapers in the other. Then she put the puppy in. Bunky sat right down and started whining, her eyes drilling into Shelby's.

"She needs something to play with," Auntie said. She gathered up an empty thread spool, a pair of rolled socks, and a piece of gray fake fur left over from a bear she'd made for Sandy. The puppy pounced on the spool, rolled to her round little back, and held it up between her paws as she chewed on it. It got away from her once, but she flipped over and captured it before it rolled out of the little pen.

Another big smile crossed Uncle's face. "I think it'll work. Boy, won't that make things easier around here?" He tweaked one of Shelby's long curls. "Now you won't have to hold that thing all the time."

"I love to hold her, Uncle, but I have to do my math

now. I have to do today's and tomorrow's too. I guess I lost my paper today."

The next day Shelby couldn't find either math paper. She remembered snapping them into the notebook. How did they get off the three rings and lost? The teacher wasn't quite so understanding as yesterday. "Your grade is in jeopardy," she said. "You must have your work made up by tomorrow."

Then Jon went on about her big, blank eyes again. This time he added some remarks that Shelby wasn't all that bright in school. All in all, the day wasn't worth bragging about.

But when she got home from cat-sitting, Auntie and Uncle were just finishing cleaning the house. They wanted Sandy to enjoy a relaxed family on her school leave.

Uncle, Auntie, and Shelby had dinner nearly ready when a car turned into the driveway. Sandy had ridden home with a friend's family. The Gobels would take both girls back Sunday afternoon.

"Here they are!" Auntie yelled and took off out the front door with Uncle and Shelby behind her.

After greeting Uncle and Auntie, Sandy turned to Shelby with tears and hugged her until it almost hurt. "I love school," she whispered into Shelby's ear, "but I miss my family too." Then she turned on a big smile. "Where's that Princess Ebony? I can't wait to meet her."

As everyone had expected, Sandy fell in love with Bunky at first sight. She had to play with the puppy for a while before they ate.

"How come Shelby got a puppy, and I didn't?" Sandy asked while they ate. She smiled at her mother. "Even if I'd gotten a puppy, it couldn't have been this cute. No way!"

The family worked together as usual after dinner to clean up the dishes and kitchen. After they finished, Sandy sat down on the couch beside Shelby. "So—how's school and band?"

Shelby hesitated. She hated to dump all over her cousin already, but she hoped for some help from her. "Well, mostly it's great. I'm in the band, and thanks to you, I can play as well as any of the kids."

Sandy leaned forward. "Do I hear a *but?*"

Shelby nodded. "One of the guys is really mean. He always makes fun of me and calls me Little Orphan Annie. He says I have big, blank eyes." She opened her eyes wide at Sandy. "Do I?"

Sandy laughed. "Of course you don't. Orphan Annie in the comics has. That's why he says that. He's just teasing you, Shelby. Probably he likes you."

Shelby swung her head back and forth. "No way. He's mean. He also says mean things about my black friend."

Uncle moved to the other end of the couch and put his hand on Shelby's shoulder. "The Bible has the answer. Remember? It says, 'Love your enemies and pray for those who persecute you.' "

"That sounds pretty hard," Shelby said. "I don't know if I could do that."

Uncle patted her arm. "Maybe we can help you."

"Hey," Sandy said, "Mom and Dad said something about adopting you. Whatever happened to that?"

Uncle and Auntie looked at Shelby but didn't reply.

"They offered," Shelby said. "I didn't know whether I should or not. But I've been thinking about it."

"The offer still goes," Uncle said. "We're ready any time you are." He and Auntie went back to the kitchen.

"I really think you should let them," Sandy said. Then she got up and started toward Shelby's room. "Come show me how much you've learned about flute playing since I left."

Shelby did, even though she hadn't progressed much since Sandy left.

After Shelby showed Sandy what she could do on the flute, the girls talked for a few minutes in Shelby's bedroom until Uncle called them to come out to the living room. When they stepped from the hall, a bunch of people jumped up and yelled "Surprise!"

LeeAnne and her mother, Shane Anderson, and two other girls from school, Jenny Duvall and Terri Phillips, seemed to fill the large living room.

Shelby felt overwhelmed. In the first place, she hardly knew Jenny and Terri. And what was the surprise all about? It couldn't be a birthday party. Her birthday was still two days away.

Then Uncle taped up a sign that said *Welcome, Bunky*.

"It's a shower for your new baby," Sandy whispered, dragging Shelby into the living room.

Shelby hardly knew what a shower was, but she knew she felt good about it. Everyone wanted to hold Bunky, so that took a while. Then they played a few games. After the games ended, Sandy took Shelby to the dining-room table, where stacks of gaily decorated gifts lay.

Shelby unwrapped soft rubber toys, leather bones, doggy treats, brushes, and many other gifts. Shane had brought a little battery-operated dog exactly the same size as Bunky. Everyone laughed and laughed watching the tiny black dog attack the yapping white toy.

Shelby could hardly believe people had gone to the trouble and expense of buying these things for her little Bunky. "Thank you, everyone," she said when she finished opening the gifts. Then she turned her eyes to Auntie and Uncle. "And thank you for doing such fantastic things for me."

Auntie moved to the table and hugged Shelby. "You're more than welcome for whatever we've done, kiddo," she said. "But this was Sandy's idea. She planned it and did most of the work from Milo. I have to agree, it was a pretty special idea."

Uncle brought in an ice-cream cake. He cut and served it to the guests, who didn't stop eating until the dessert was gone. Bunky got a small piece too.

Shelby especially thanked Jenny and Terri for coming and asked them how they came to be there.

"Our big sisters are Sandy's friends," Jenny said. "She wrote and asked us, and we accepted. That's it."

Shelby still felt excited after everyone left. "I can't believe you did this," she kept repeating to the family. "A shower for a dog? Thank you."

Finally she remembered Molly hadn't been there. "Did you forget to invite Molly?" she asked Auntie.

Aunt Rachel shook her head. "I called one night after you'd gone to bed and got her father. He told me in plain language what he thought of a shower for a dog. And that his daughter wouldn't be involved."

The family had an extra-long worship that night because Sandy had two stories she wanted to read to Shelby. Both were about dogs. In one the dog rescued a child, and in the other a child rescued a dog—both with God's obvious help.

In bed, Shelby thanked God for giving her such a fantastic aunt, uncle, and cousin. She especially thanked Him for Bunky. Then her mind turned to Molly. Although Molly wouldn't admit it, Shelby knew she felt bad about being left out.

The next day at school, Shelby told LeeAnne the Bible said they had to be nice to Jon, no matter what he said or did. LeeAnne agreed.

And after keeping her notebook in her arms all day, Shelby handed in her math papers for three days.

In band, Jon started on his Little Orphan Annie thing again. Shelby did her very best not to hear a word, but by the time he got to the part about her blank eyes, LeeAnne lost control. "You're just making a fool of yourself, Jon!" she shouted. "Shelby lives in a super-nice house and has a great family. She's probably a lot luckier than you. She even has a darling puppy of her very own. So shut up, OK?"

Jon looked surprised for a moment, then laughed out loud. "Of course!" he yelled. "It's name is Sandy, isn't it?"

Just then, Mrs. Beecher walked in, and she had a frown on her face. "Is something wrong?" she asked. "It seems like the past couple of days, every time I walk in here, somebody's shouting angry words. Can anyone explain that?"

Mrs. Beecher looked out over the classroom, but no one said a word. She stood for a moment, waiting. Then she picked up some music. "I hope it doesn't happen again," she said softly. "Let's get on with our practice."

CHAPTER

5

A Birthday Bike

S helby thoroughly enjoyed her band period that day. And Jon didn't say anything else awful to either her or LeeAnne.

Sandy's time at home went fast. The family attended church together. Shelby enjoyed Sabbath School now that she didn't feel so strange. She didn't speak up, though, the way some of the other kids did.

Saturday night the family had a little birthday party for Shelby. They gave her a metallic-red ten-speed bicycle.

"Oh, thank you," she said. "I'm so happy, I don't know what to say! But I was saving my cat-sitting money for a bike."

Uncle tweaked a curl. "You'll find something to spend that on," he said.

"Yeah," Aunt Rachel said. "We're just trying to save

you from that wild run to the lake. Imagine having to run as fast as someone else rides a bike!"

Shelby laughed. "I really like the bike, Aunt Rachel. It's a lot nicer than I'd have bought. But you know what? Molly puffs harder than I do after our trip to the lake. In fact, she makes me wait for her sometimes."

That night Sandy asked Shelby if she could sleep with Bunky. Of course, Shelby let her. She thought she might enjoy being able to sleep all through a night again. But she kept waking up—only to find Bunky gone.

The next morning the family enjoyed a big country breakfast together. Later in the day they had to take Sandy and her friend Wendy Phillips back to Milo Academy.

Shelby had a great time—except for the three times Bunky barfed on her. Auntie assured her the puppy would get used to riding as she grew older and stop throwing up. But that didn't clean the smell from Shelby's clothes.

That night at worship Uncle started his prayer by asking God to bless Jon Greenflower and help him with his problems.

The next day as Shelby walked to the bus with Molly, she told her about her new red bike. Molly didn't seem nearly as excited as Shelby thought she'd be.

"You didn't need a bike," Molly said. "Now I'll never be able to keep up with you. It's because you're so big, Shelby." (With Molly's lisp the last sentence sounded like, "It'th becauth you're tho big.")

Shelby laughed. "I won't run away from you, Molly. Can we go for a ride this afternoon?"

Molly stopped walking. "I thought you never had time anymore," she said. "First you baby-sit the dumb cats; then you play with your dog and practice. Then you play with your dog again. You tell me, Shelby, do you have time to ride a bike?"

A half-smile grew on Shelby's face. "I am pretty busy, aren't I?" she agreed. She felt good about being busy.

That afternoon after school was out, she and Molly rode to the lake, rested a little while on the bank, and then rode back. After Molly went home, Shelby rode her bike back to the lake and home again. She flew like the wind, and the ride felt as smooth and quiet as the wind too. She'd never expected to have a bike like that. Neither had she ever expected to have a dog like Bunky.

And her family wasn't too bad, either. Pedaling along the paved road, she felt a quiet glow of happiness. "Thank You, Jesus," she whispered. "The Bible says You'll turn our sorrow to joy, and You've really done that for me. Thank You. I love You."

The next day, when Shelby took her seat in English class, she spotted one of her missing math papers on the floor beside her desk. Black sneaker tracks smudged the neatly worked-out problems. Leaning over the edge of the desk, she retrieved it. As she sat back up, she felt something slide across her other arm. A quick glance revealed the other math paper in a long, lean hand covered with blond hairs.

Her eyes lifted to meet Jon's. He laughed out loud as she tried to snatch it from his hand. "How did you get these?" she yelled.

He shrugged, still laughing. "I found them," he said.

"What use would Little Orphan Annie have with math papers?"

Shelby felt her face grow hot and the cords in her throat tighten. She opened her mouth to tell him exactly what she thought of him. Then she remembered the Bible's advice: "Pray for those who persecute you."

She swallowed hard. "Help me, Jesus." Then with a forced smile she handed him the paper she'd retrieved from the floor. "Here," she said softly. "The papers are twins and should stay together."

Jon's eyes opened wide, and his mouth dropped open. For a second he stood like a statue. Then he took the papers and returned to his own seat.

Shelby leaned her forehead on her hands, thinking. It worked! "Thank You, Lord Jesus." She smiled and pulled out her English book.

A few days later Shelby hurried into the house after spending her usual hour with the cats, King Tut and Princess.

"Your dog isn't satisfied in the pen anymore," Auntie said after Shelby had greeted her and lifted Bunky from the pen. "We're going to have to fix the kitchen so she can be in there part of the time." She smiled at Shelby. "I've never seen a dog like this that couldn't stand to be away from people."

Shelby helped Aunt Rachel fix dinner. Then Uncle James used a window screen and a big piece of cardboard he had found in the garage to block the two kitchen doors. "Put her down," Uncle said to Shelby when he finished. "Let's see if she likes it."

Shelby put the puppy down, and she made a puddle

on the floor. "Oops," Shelby said. "Should I put her back into her pen?"

"I'll mix up some disinfectant spray," Auntie said, "while you clean up the puddle. Then we'll put some newspapers in the corner. She isn't doing so well in her playpen, either. Hopefully she'll catch on pretty soon."

Bunky kept right on wetting everywhere. But she never wet Shelby's bed. Not once.

Finally Thanksgiving came, and so did Sandy. Shelby enjoyed every minute of the vacation, but soon they drove Sandy and her friend back to Milo. The next day Shelby found herself back in school again.

The first afternoon back, Shelby's choir teacher, Miss Johns, announced in choir class that for the Christmas program this year they would sing an operetta. She had written it herself and already had the lead parts chosen. Because Molly was so short, she would be the poor little girl who had no family or home. Because Shelby was so tall, she would play the part of the rich young matron who befriended the child. Jon Greenflower, the tallest boy, would be Shelby's husband, who tried to prevent his wife from bringing the dirty urchin into their home.

"I've chosen each of you," Miss Hunt told the choir, "because you sing well and will be able to learn the songs. You also have the ability to act the parts."

Shelby's heart dropped right into her shoes when she learned that Jon would be *her* husband. Hadn't he given her enough trouble without her spending time practicing the play with him? She held up her hand. "I have an after-school job. I won't be able to stay."

The teacher smiled and pushed back a short, dark

curl. "We'll practice during school time—and maybe a few lunch recesses. I'm sure you'll all enjoy this little thing I've written. It's mostly funny, but it still makes us stop and remember what Christmas is all about. Any other problems?"

Jonathan Greenflower's hand went up. "No one can understand Molly," he said loudly. Then he laughed. "Haven't you noticed how she talks?"

Shelby glanced at Molly and saw bright red color creep over her face. She drew in a breath of sympathy for Molly, knowing how it felt to be on the receiving end of Jon's sharp tongue.

"Molly's lisp makes her a natural for the part," Miss Johns said. "And I don't have any trouble understanding her. Can you understand her all right, class?" Everyone yelled Yes.

Miss Johns assigned the rest of the parts. Those who didn't get speaking parts would form a small choir, which would do many numbers. Then she handed out the parts. "Familiarize yourself with the words, and we'll start learning the music tomorrow." The teacher looked pretty with her rosy cheeks and wide smile.

Shelby didn't get a chance to say any more, but she thought about it a lot during the day. The play looked fun, and she'd love to do it. But why did Jon have to be involved? Of course, he'd make it miserable for her. When she walked into the band room that afternoon, she discovered that Jon had been thinking about the operetta too. "I understand how much it would mean to you to be my wife," he yelled. "But how could you expect to learn all those songs with your big, blank eyes?"

Shelby wanted to tell him that her eyes could learn anything faster than his. But she didn't. "It sounds fun, and I'm going to try," she said in the most civilized voice she could scare up.

"Well, I know you'll embarrass me by never learning anything."

CHAPTER

6

Molly Hates Jon

That evening Molly and Shelby dressed Bunky in pajamas. "Either she's getting bigger, or the clothes are getting smaller," Shelby said. "Let's weigh her." Molly pulled off the clothes and picked Bunky up.

They put the puppy on an old baby scales that Shelby had found in a corner of her closet shortly after she moved in. They discovered that Bunky had gained four ounces since the last time Shelby had weighed her.

"That's not enough to make the clothes smaller," Molly said. "Anyway, let's look at the Christmas program." So they went over the whole thing together. When they finished, Molly squirmed and looked into Shelby's eyes. "Do you think I can do it?" she asked, so quietly that it almost came out a whisper.

Shelby laughed, cuddling Bunky close and stroking

her nose. "Of course, you can do it. You didn't hear that jerk give me a bad time in band. If I can do it, you *sure* can. We just have to ignore him, Molly."

Bunky liked being loose in the kitchen as long as someone was in there with her. But she couldn't stand being alone, ever, anywhere.

Two nights later Shelby helped clean up the kitchen as usual. Then she tried to relax in a recliner in the living room. But her puppy stood propped against the cardboard barrier, crying. "I'm right here, dolly," Shelby called. Only the breakfast bar separated the kitchen from the living room. "I gave you some of your toys, Bunk. Can't you play with them?"

Just then Shelby heard a small crash, and Bunky appeared in the living room. "Oh, oh," she said, putting the footrest down and jumping to her feet. "You can't be on the carpet. You'd love to wet on it—or worse." She hurried toward her puppy. But for the first time ever, the dog ran from Shelby. She called softly and moved toward Bunky again. This time the dog ran behind the couch. Shelby began to panic. Uncle and Auntie would definitely not be pleased if the dog had an accident on the carpet. But every time she got close to the dog, it dashed around or behind a piece of furniture.

"What's going on in here? It looks as if you girls are having fun," Uncle said from the hall.

Shelby dashed after her puppy once more. Then she noticed. Bunky *was* having fun! When Shelby stopped, the dog ran almost up to her. When Shelby ran after her, she flew like the wind around some piece of furniture.

Shelby looked up at her uncle. "Could you help me,

Uncle? I can't catch her alone. She has too many places to hide."

Uncle stood there, laughing. "Her four-wheel drive is in great working order," he said. "She cuts corners in a second. And did you notice how her fur flows behind as she flashes around?"

Shelby watched the dog a moment. "Uncle! Help me," she pleaded. "She's going to have an accident on the carpet."

Finally, with his help, Shelby caught the dog. "You bad little thing," she murmured into her puppy's ear. "When you learn to be a big girl, you can run free." She carried the puppy to her playpen, gave her a big kiss on the side of her nose, and gently put her in. Then she put a soft little ball in for Bunky to chew on.

Uncle checked the fallen piece of cardboard. "I'll have to secure this a little better," he said. "Maybe I'll put some heavy magazines behind it." He grinned at Shelby. "Did you notice that we didn't catch her until she wanted to be caught? I can't believe a two-and-a-half-month-old, one-pound dog could run like that."

"One-and-a-quarter pounds," Shelby corrected. When Uncle looked puzzled, she said, "Molly and I weighed her earlier this evening."

"One-and-a-quarter pounds," Uncle said solemnly.

A few afternoons later, Shelby managed to get her chores finished earlier than usual. The sun shone outside. It was a cool but beautiful December day. "Do you think Molly and I could take a bike ride before dark?" she asked Auntie, who had just come into the kitchen from the office.

Auntie checked her watch. "You have less than an

hour," she said. "You should be able to take a short one. Why don't you call her?"

Shelby decided to just go over. It had been a long time since she'd talked to Molly's folks. Maybe things were better over there now. As she braked in Molly's driveway, she wished she'd called. Her heart pounded with fear. She put the kickstand down, marched up the front steps, and rang the doorbell.

Molly's stepmother Aggie opened the door six inches. "What do you want?" she asked.

Shelby swallowed. "It's such a nice day, I wondered if Molly could take a little ride with me?"

"No, she can't." Slam.

Shelby flew back down the porch steps and jumped on her bicycle. Somehow she'd lost interest in a bike ride, but she rode up and down Marina Drive, thinking about Molly. With Molly living across the road, Shelby could never feel sorry for herself. Even losing a mother didn't compare to Molly's problems. But that's exactly what had happened to Molly! She'd lost her mother too. And she hadn't lucked out as Shelby had. Once again Shelby thanked God for her good home. And for good measure she thanked Him for her puppy—again.

A few days later Shelby received a letter with a check for $100.00 from the vacationing Strattons. The letter said $77.50 was for cat-sitting and the rest for food. Sometimes she got tired of spending an hour over there every day, but where else could she ever earn money like that? Now she had lots of money for Christmas shopping.

Shelby loved practicing the Christmas operetta, and she'd have enjoyed working on it immensely if Jon hadn't bothered her so much. He figured a way to make her life miserable every single day. But no matter what he did, Shelby ignored it.

One day as they finished practicing, he grabbed Shelby's shoulders. "I'd be a mean husband if I didn't kiss my wife once in a while," he whispered. He jerked her close, spit in her face, and ran off, laughing.

"I'll get him for that, somehow," Shelby fumed. Then she stopped and thought. No. She couldn't do that. She had to love him. She shook her head. She *would* get him! Sometimes she didn't feel much like a Christian. She hurried to the restroom and washed her face with soap and warm water. She still felt dirty as she rushed into her math class late.

Bunky seemed perfectly satisfied living in the kitchen as long as someone was with her. As soon as everyone left, she tried to break out. And she succeeded about once every day. Whenever that happened, the whole family had a merry chase catching her.

"I'm sure that dog enjoys being chased," Auntie said one day after they'd spent ten minutes chasing her all through the living and dining rooms. Bunky would run behind something when they got too close. Then she'd run almost into their hands, then zap away again.

"She wins a double bonus," Uncle said. "She escapes from the kitchen, and she also gets a good run. Of course, she likes it!"

"It's time for Bunky's second shot," Auntie said one day when Shelby came home from school. "Would you like to go?"

Shelby didn't want her baby to be hurt, but if she had to have the shots, Shelby wanted to be with her.

A half-hour later Shelby and Aunt Rachel were answering questions at the animal hospital. "The dog's name?" the receptionist asked.

"Bu—I mean Princess Ebony," Shelby replied.

The woman nodded and wrote on her form. "Do you call her Princess or Ebony? Or both?"

Auntie laughed. "She answers to Bunky."

A few minutes later, Shelby stood beside the shiny examining table while the kind vet carefully inserted the needle into the skin in the back of Bunky's neck. The dog barely squeaked. "She may not feel very frisky for a few days," the doctor said. "Just keep her comfortable and quiet. Bring her back in a month for her last shot."

That evening the puppy burst out of the kitchen twice and had a merry time as the three of them chased her around the furniture. Finally she tired and let Shelby pick her up. "You didn't listen when the doctor said you wouldn't feel well," Shelby whispered to her little friend. The shot didn't affect the puppy at all as far as anyone could tell.

Shelby had learned all her songs for the Christmas program by the end of the first week. She remembered not long ago when singing alone would have scared her to death. God and her new family definitely gave her confidence. Except for Jon's cruel and crude antics, she dearly loved practicing for the Christmas program.

He tormented Molly too. One day Molly had trouble with the melody in one of her solos. "Miss Johns, could you sing it with me a couple more times?" she finally asked.

"Mith Johnth," Jon mimicked, "could you thing it

with me a couple more timeth?" He did a more pro-
nounced lisp than Molly, and it really did sound funny.
Most of the kids laughed.

Tears burst into Molly's eyes. She jumped from her
chair and began screaming. "I hate you, Jonathan
Greenflower. You're the meanetht perthon I've ever
known." She put her face in her hands and sobbed a
moment. Then she looked at him again. "I hope you die
tomorrow. I hope a takthi cab runth over you and
thmatheth you into the thtreet. [I hope a taxi cab runs
over you and smashes you into the street.]"

CHAPTER
7
Training Bunky

M iss Johns hadn't noticed Jon making fun, but when Molly started screaming, her head jerked away from the student she'd been helping. "Molly, stop that right now," she said in a firm voice. "It's all right to get mad sometimes, but it's never all right to wish someone dead." She stood up, looked at the clock, and dismissed the class.

Shelby followed Molly to the restroom. Molly dropped onto a chair, sobbing hard. "I'm never going back into that room," she said. Shelby absently noticed that Molly had just said a whole sentence without an *s*, so she hadn't lisped.

Shelby put her arms around Molly as she sat on the chair and tried to comfort her. "You have to be tough," she whispered into Molly's hair when the sobbing subsided. "He picks on me because I'm an orphan. The

Bible says I have to love him. Auntie and Uncle tell me I have to ignore him, or he'll do it all the more. Do you think you could ignore him?"

The tear-streaked face jerked sideways so fast that her pale blond curls wiped some tears away. "I could never ignore him. Never in my whole life."

Shelby tried to pull Molly up. "Come on. We'll be late for class."

Two more sobs. "I'm not going to class."

"I have to go, Molly. Are you coming?" Molly shook her head, so Shelby took off down the hall toward her classroom. She almost wished Jon were dead too, but she knew she didn't want to hold on to that feeling. The Bible said to love our enemies and pray for those who are mean to us. She prayed for Jon every night with Uncle and Auntie and tried to be nice to him.

Later, as the girls walked down Marina Drive toward their houses, they talked. "Why don't you tell your dad about Jon?" Shelby asked.

Molly snorted. "My dad would only yell at me," she said. "He'd tell me it was all my fault, and I'd better shape up. Right now he's mad because he has to take me to the Christmas program. If I cause any trouble, he'll jerk me out of the operetta."

Nothing was done about Jon, mostly, Shelby decided, because he nearly always managed to say mean things and pull mean tricks when the teachers weren't around or weren't looking. Somehow, though, the Christmas program gradually took shape. Shelby told Miss Johns how much she liked the operetta and how much she admired the teacher for being able to write it. In return, Miss Johns told Shelby she had a beautiful voice and that she really should take voice lessons.

A week before Christmas, Sandy arrived home. The family bought and trimmed a large Christmas tree. Sandy took Shelby Christmas shopping while the girls caught each other up on their doings. Sandy's enthusiasm made holiday preparations much more exciting.

Finally the day of the program arrived. Shelby rushed home wrapped in a pink cloud of excitement. Unlike Molly's family, everyone in her family seemed eager for the evening program.

As she practiced her flute that afternoon, Shelby had an idea. "Auntie," she called as she ran into the office, "could Molly ride with us? Her dad isn't happy about having to take her."

"Whatever you want, kiddo," Aunt Rachel said. "Her folks should be proud of her part in the operetta and eager to go. But they aren't about to do what we think they should. Invite her if you want."

Shelby took a deep breath before dialing the number. Her stepmother or dad hardly ever let her talk to Molly. "Hello," Molly's dad's coarse voice said.

"Hello, Mr. Lindstrum. Could I talk to Molly, please?"

"She's busy. Don't you know tonight's the stupid program?"

"I know. That's what I need to talk to her about."

He snorted out a nasty-sounding laugh. "It may be, but I'll bet it can wait until tonight." He hung up, and the dial tone buzzed. Shelby pulled the receiver away from her ear and looked at it. How could anyone be so mean?

The Gobel family drove into the school parking lot at seven o'clock that evening, a half-hour before the program was to begin.

When Shelby climbed out of the car, she found Mr. Lindstrum leaning against his pickup, smoking a cigarette. "Well," he said, when he saw Shelby, "I see you made it without talking to Molly. I guess it did keep, didn't it?"

Shelby looked into his eyes and shook her head. "No, sir, I'm afraid it didn't. I called to invite Molly to ride with us."

He gave her a strange look. "You idiot," he snapped. "You could have said that to me."

Suddenly Shelby laughed. "You scared me so bad that I didn't think of it." She didn't add that she was nearly that scared right now, talking to him face to face.

"Come on, Shelby," Uncle called, coming around to see what was holding her up.

"Uncle," Shelby said, "this is Molly's dad, Mr. Lindstrum."

"Well, hello, neighbor," Uncle said, extending his hand. The man ignored Uncle's friendly gesture. "We'd better be getting you inside," Uncle James said to Shelby. Then he turned back to the man leaning against the pickup. "Are you alone? Would you like to sit with us?"

The man swore softly, though not at Uncle. "I'm not going in there," he said. "Why would anyone want to watch a bunch of dumb kids making fools of themselves?"

"I don't think that's going to happen," Uncle said. "The teacher knows her stuff, and it'll be well worth seeing." He turned to Shelby. "Let's go, Shelby. I can't tell you how much I'm looking forward to this program." Shelby could tell he'd said it loud enough for Mr. Lindstrum to hear. She felt a big wave of love for Uncle James. Then she remembered she'd soon be singing alone—in front of ten zillion people. As she stepped into the gym with her family, the only thing she thought about was how scared she felt.

But later, as the operetta progressed, she could tell it was going well, and she felt less frightened. And as she felt calmer, she could hear her voice growing stronger and truer. Then it was over, and Jon hadn't done anything horrible. The audience clapped, whistled, and screamed its appreciation.

Shelby rode home in a rosy glow.

"I didn't realize you could sing like that," Sandy said.

"Neither did I," Uncle repeated.

"Hey, kiddo," Aunt Rachel added. "Your teacher suggested you should have voice lessons. How does that sound?"

For a second it sounded great to Shelby. And she felt all warm inside that Uncle James and Aunt Rachel would pay for lessons for her. Then she remembered the cats. And her flute. And Bunky. And Molly. Molly really did need her. "I don't know, Auntie. I'm already pretty busy."

Auntie reached an arm into the dark back seat, found Shelby's arm, and patted it. "Maybe later you won't feel so pressured."

Shelby's best Christmas came and went. She told herself it wasn't best because she got so many gifts. It was best because she had a whole family to share her happiness with.

Sandy gave her two of her very favorite presents—

books. One told everything there is to know about Pomeranians and their care. The other explained how to train a dog for showing.

"You are planning to show Bunky, aren't you?" Sandy asked after the Christmas tree had been picked bare. "I can't think of any other reason to buy such a fancy dog." Then she glanced at the tiny animal in the playpen. Bunky lay on her back, contentedly playing with a soft rubber teddy bear. A smile formed on Sandy's face. "On second thought, I can't imagine how anyone could resist buying her."

"I'd love to show her," Shelby gushed. "But I don't know how."

Sandy laughed. "Good. That's what the book's for."

Shelby and Molly rode bikes a lot during Christmas vacation. Molly rode while her dad and stepmother worked. Shelby rode just a little faster than Molly, and Molly seemed to ride a little faster than before.

Sandy helped Shelby on the flute every day while Auntie worked in the office. Uncle had to go to work too. Shelby learned more from Sandy in one day than in a month at school.

One cold sunny afternoon Sandy and Shelby got bored. "Think you could find the Pomeranian farm where you got your dog?" Sandy asked. "Why don't you take me to see it?"

With permission from Auntie, a half-hour later, the girls turned into the farmhouse driveway. Emil came out and noticed Bunky in Shelby's arms. "Well, she turned out right pretty," he said in his soft, kindly voice.

Shelby showed Bunky her yapping, cream-colored mother, Misty Rose, and her coal-black father, Ricochet Bullet. The tiny puppy pressed hard against Shelby's chest. She refused to even look at the noisy animals. "She doesn't like your dogs," Shelby said to Emil, but the dogs were raising such a racket that he didn't hear her.

"Do you have any puppies now?" Sandy asked.

The man shook his head. "Nobody's even expectin' right now." Then he grinned. "Come spring, though, we'll have lots of little ones. Were you wanting one?"

Shelby moved closer. She'd love for Sandy to get one. But Sandy shook her head. "Not right now, I'm afraid. I go to boarding school and won't be around much until school's out. Your dogs are beautiful, though."

That evening Shelby started studying one of her new books: *How to Train and Show Your Dog.* The next day she began training Bunky. "You're supposed to stand still," she explained to the puppy as she stood the dog on the bathroom counter. Every time she released the baby, it started to jump around. "Stand," Shelby repeated gently a dozen times, holding her still. After ten minutes, Bunky seemed to catch on a little and stood where Shelby placed her. Then Shelby cuddled her close. "You're such a good baby," she cooed. "But the book said not to try to teach you for more than ten minutes a day. So now you get to play in your little playpen again."

Shelby worked with her baby ten minutes every day, and the puppy seemed to catch on a little more each time.

Then the Christmas vacation ended, and Sandy had to go back to school. Shelby did too.

"Can you spend the night with me tomorrow night?" LeeAnne asked on the second day of school.

Jon did his trick in band again that afternoon. "Here comes Little Orphan Annie," he bellowed when Shelby came through the door. "Check that red hair." He leaned over and made exaggerated motions of looking around her feet. "And Sandy. Where's that dumb dog I keep hearing about?"

Shelby managed to work up a laugh. "Come on, Jon," she said in a light, friendly voice. "We all know you can do better than that."

Just then, Mrs. Beecher came in, and everyone started warming up and tuning. When they tried to play, the teacher stopped them. "You saxes sound perfectly awful," she wailed.

She worked with the saxophones for what seemed forever. *Those kids should be in a beginner's band*, Shelby thought. Then she chuckled. What did she think this was, anyway? No one was exactly professional. Shelby grew more and more bored waiting for class to continue. It seemed that lately, band period had turned into a special class for the saxes. Why couldn't those kids practice at home like she did?

Suddenly something wet and cold plopped against her cheek. Checking the floor, she discovered a sloppy spitball beside her shoe. She turned around just in time to catch another one right between her eyes. That was too much. She jumped up and charged toward Jon. "If you do that again, I'm going to pound your head into the floor," she yelled at him. Then she rushed back and dropped into her seat, wishing she'd kept quiet. Now he'd be meaner than ever. She knew he would. Besides that, she'd hurt Jesus.

Shelby's outburst broke the teacher's concentration

on the saxophones. "What's this all about?" she demanded, looking straight at Shelby. "Who did what?"

Shelby could feel the red color rising from her neck to her face. Why had she lost her temper? Why had she said those mean words?

LeeAnne spoke up. "Jon Greenflower keeps tormenting Shelby," she said. "He calls her 'Little Orphan Annie,' and he steals her homework and hides it. This time he threw a wad of paper covered with spit in her face."

There was a long pause. "Is that true, Shelby?" Mrs. Beecher asked quietly.

Shelby slid down in her chair and wished she could sink into the floor. Why had she created such a scene?

"Is it?" Mrs. Beecher asked again.

Shelby nodded.

"Jonathan Greenflower, I want you to talk to you after class," she said. "The rest of you are dismissed."

CHAPTER

8

Clothes
Decorate the Hall

Of course, you can spend the night with LeeAnne," Aunt Rachel said that afternoon when Shelby asked. "I'm glad you've found a nice friend like her."

"What about Bunky? Shall I take her?"

Auntie shook her dark head. "You'd have to take her playpen too. We wouldn't want her having accidents at LeeAnne's place." She looked troubled for just a second. "I wish that little rascal would stop wetting everywhere. Anyway, I'll take good care of her. She can even sleep with us. And you can take care of the cats tomorrow morning before you go to school, then Thursday afternoon when you get home. They'll be just fine."

"What about Bunky's training?"

Aunt Rachel smiled. "She'll still remember what you've been doing if you skip a day. Stop worrying, kiddo. Just go."

Shelby called LeeAnne, and both girls rejoiced.

The next day Molly didn't meet Shelby to walk to the bus. Shelby waited five minutes, then raced over to Molly's porch. She took a deep breath. Why did she keep coming over here, anyway? She'd probably get run off.

But no one answered the door. Then Shelby noticed both cars gone from the driveway. She tried the door, which wasn't locked, then opened it a little. "Molly!" she bellowed.

"Come in," a small voice called from the direction of Molly's bedroom. As Shelby moved through the living room toward Molly's room, she noticed a tall vase of cattails. It hadn't been there the last time she'd been inside this place. That had been way back last summer when Molly had cut her foot. Her folks hadn't taken her to the doctor, and it had been awful.

She turned into Molly's open door. Sure enough, Molly lay in her bed. Her face looked white and her eyes red. "What's the matter?" Shelby asked.

Molly shook her tangled hair. "I don't feel good," she said. Her voice sounded hoarse. "Don't get too close."

Shelby stepped back two steps. "Are you alone?"

Molly nodded.

Shelby didn't know exactly what to do. She knew she had to get to school, though. "Well, I hope you feel better," she said, easing toward the door. "I have to get going."

When she reached the road, she decided she'd better tell Aunt Rachel. Maybe she could take Molly something for lunch. "Auntie," she yelled, racing into the house, "could you check Molly sometime? She's sick."

Aunt Rachel hurried from the office. "What's wrong with her?" she asked, puffing just a little.

Shelby shook her head. "She sounds hoarse and looks awful."

Auntie checked the clock. "And you've missed the bus, young lady. What do you propose to do about that?"

Shelby hung her head. "I'm sorry. I didn't mean to. Could I ride my bike? It's only a couple of miles."

Aunt Rachel bit her lip, looking undecided. "There's lots of traffic on the road to school. Why don't I just take you?"

The ride to school was short. After thanking Auntie, Shelby walked into the school five minutes before the bus came. "I brought my stuff," she yelled when LeeAnne arrived. She held up the plastic bag of clothes and other things. "I get to spend the night." The excited girls jabbered so fast and long that Shelby forgot to put her things in the locker. Oh, well, she could do that later. She shoved the bag under her desk and pulled out her English book.

Near the end of the period Shelby carried her completed essay to the teacher's desk. She'd done a good job on it, and she felt satisfied.

When the bell rang, LeeAnne rushed to her again. "My mom said she'd fix a special supper tonight. And we get to watch a Disney movie and make popcorn."

She hugged Shelby's arm. "I'm so glad you're coming."

"So am I," Shelby said. "I haven't been with anyone overnight since I came to Veneta." Then she remembered her bag of stuff. "I'd better put my things away," she said, reaching under her seat to pick it up. When she didn't touch it, she felt around a little more. Then she leaned over and looked. "The bag's gone!" She looked around for Jon, who wasn't in the room.

"Where is he?" she whispered, almost crying. "Where is that jerk?"

The girls ran into the hall, and Shelby found her things strung from one end of the hall to the other. Clean jeans and a T-shirt, socks and underwear, hairbrush and toothbrush. Everything. Shelby felt her face getting hot. "Help me, LeeAnne," she begged, "before anyone else sees." Both girls started gathering things into their arms. Finally Shelby grabbed her little bear and wrapped it inside her T-shirt.

"I'll bet you sleep with that," LeeAnne said with a smile. "Come on, Shelby, this isn't the end of the world. Everyone wears underwear."

Shelby managed a shaky smile. "But they don't decorate the school halls with it. I *hate* Jon Greenflower! I really do." Unable to find the plastic bag she'd brought the clothes in, Shelby carried the things in her arms to her locker. "There," she said, shoving the stuff inside. "That'll be fun to gather up later."

Getting herself back together, she fired a wide grin at LeeAnne. "Don't tell me the Bible says I can't hate people, either. I already know it."

"Don't say anything to him," LeeAnne warned. "If he did it, he won't be able to keep quiet about it."

Jon didn't say a word to Shelby the rest of the day, and she didn't say anything to him, either.

Then school dismissed, and both girls boarded LeeAnne's bus. Shelby felt excited as she and LeeAnne jumped from the bus and took off running down a quiet lane. The houses were all nice and the yards neat, and when they reached LeeAnne's house, the windows, walks, and porches looked cleaner than any house Shelby had ever seen.

"I like your place," she told LeeAnne.

LeeAnne opened the door. "Mom," she called, "we're here."

Mrs. Burton came from somewhere down the hall. Her shiny black hair had a gentle wave and turned under at the bottom. Shelby could see right off where LeeAnne got her huge black eyes. Her mother's eyes had the same laughing look too. But Shelby noticed a question in them.

"Hello, Mrs. Burton," she said. "Your place is beautiful. It looks as if someone loves it."

The woman relaxed before Shelby's eyes, and her full lips curved into a laugh. "Well, we all take our turns loving it. Sometimes the kids object, but we do it anyway."

That evening at the supper table, Shelby met LeeAnne's dad and her twin sisters Marjie and Katie. The girls were several years younger than LeeAnne. Shelby noticed that they seemed to hold her in awe, and she smiled to herself. She couldn't imagine anyone holding *her* in awe!

Mr. Burton interrupted Shelby's thoughts. "I hear you like our place," he said.

"I do," Shelby replied. "It's so clean, it sparkles, even on the outside."

Mrs. Burton sighed. "We just wish our neighbors felt that way."

Shelby swallowed her bite of stuffed baked potato. "How could they feel different? It's the most attractive place in the neighborhood."

"We've lived here four years," Mr. Burton said. "We've never been invited into a single home. But every year we get at least a dozen invitations to move. They say we're ruining the real-estate value of the neighborhood."

Instantly, Shelby heard Jon saying that she hung around with LeeAnne only because the white kids didn't like her. Mom had never acted as though black people were different from white people, and neither did Uncle and Auntie.

Shelby felt shocked.

CHAPTER

9

Molly's Mean Dad

I don't see how they could think you'd hurt the property values," Shelby said. "Your place is the nicest in the neighborhood."

Mrs. Burton laughed bitterly. "It's not the condition of the house. It's the color of our skin."

Later Shelby lay awake clutching her bear. It wasn't even a poor substitute for Bunky, but she held it anyway. Hearing LeeAnne's quiet snores, she thought about the Burton family. It would be truly awful if your neighbors didn't want you around. She clutched the bear tighter.

"Dear God," she whispered, "could You help the Burtons to have life a little easier? And help me realize that just because I lost Mom, I'm not the only one with problems. Be sure to watch over Bunky and Sandy. And help me be a Christian to Jon Greenflower. Bless him too. Good night, Father. I love You."

The next afternoon when Shelby greeted her dog, she noticed the puppy looked different. Putting Bunky on the bathroom counter, she told her to "stand." After studying the puppy a moment, she grabbed it into her arms. "Auntie," she yelled, running to the office. "Bunky's lost most of her hair."

Auntie appeared with a large smile on her face. She reached for Shelby and hugged her tightly. "I'm glad to see you too, kiddo. We missed you a lot. So did Bunky." Then she ran her hand down the pup's back as Shelby held it. "Yep. I've been noticing that our little show dog is becoming short-haired fast."

Shelby's heart lodged somewhere in her throat. "Is she all right?"

Aunt Rachel laughed. "Of course, she's all right. Let's just hope she doesn't get completely bald like baby people do sometimes." Then she raised her dark eyebrows. "Bunky will also lose her baby teeth soon."

"Kids do that too, don't they?" Relieved about her dog, Shelby worked with her awhile.

Later Shelby told Auntie and Uncle about the Burtons and how their neighbors didn't like them.

Uncle nodded thoughtfully. "They're right," he said. "People think racial discrimination is past, but it isn't. Most blacks are still persecuted." He put his chin in his hands and looked sad for a moment. "It's ridiculous for anyone to think he's better than another because of skin color," he muttered. Then he raised his eyes to Aunt Rachel's. "Why don't we invite the Burtons over?"

"I'd love that," Shelby said. "I'll help get ready."

Aunt Rachel nodded, deep in thought. "I'd like that

too. Right now, I have another problem. Molly's pretty sick, Shelby. If you were that sick, I'd take you to a doctor. Her folks don't even leave lunch for her."

"What are you thinking?" Shelby asked.

Auntie shrugged. "I'm wondering if we should talk to her folks."

"I didn't find her father very sympathetic," Uncle said. "Could you keep taking lunch to her another day or two and see how she does?"

Aunt Rachel nodded. "Sure. I take her a big pitcher of orange juice every day too. Maybe she'll get better."

"You won't let her die, will you?" Shelby asked.

Auntie hugged her again. "She's not that sick. But I'll be watching her."

Shelby spent extra time working with Bunky that night. She tried to teach her to "stay." Bunky seemed eager to learn to be a show dog, but she still had accidents on the carpet. Shelby took her to her paper every half-hour, but sometimes the puppy didn't wait even that long. Following the dog-care book, Shelby didn't spank her but showed her the puddle and said "No!" very firmly.

At family worship that night, everyone prayed for Molly and also the Burtons. Then, with Bunky cuddling close, Shelby prayed for both in her own little prayer session in bed. She also prayed for Jon to be nice.

The next day Jon came and sat down at the lunch table with LeeAnne and Shelby. "What do you want?" LeeAnne asked.

Jon grinned. Then he turned to Shelby. "I just wondered what color they are today," he said mysteriously. "Could they be white lace? Or maybe they're red bikini. What are they, Shelby?"

"What are what?" Shelby asked. Then it hit her. Her underwear! The underwear that had been scattered over the hall. Her face burned. What a jerk! She grabbed LeeAnne's hand. "I'm through. Let's get out of here."

LeeAnne jerked up her tray, put her dishes on it, and they took off.

Shelby dragged LeeAnne to the restroom. They washed up, then sat down on the couch. Suddenly Shelby began laughing. "Well, I thought of something to be thankful for," she said finally. "If I'd been living with my mother, the underwear would have been full of holes and runs. Jon would have loved that."

"Yeah," LeeAnne said. "And now we know for sure he's the guy who stole it."

Then Shelby told her they were going to invite the Burtons over to visit. Both girls hoped it would be soon.

Running home from the bus that afternoon, Shelby wished she didn't have to cat-sit every day. It took a lot of her time. She'd much rather spend the time on voice lessons. Auntie had never said any more about lessons, and neither had she suggested that Shelby quit caring for the cats. That must mean they wanted her to keep on. So she would. After all, they did a lot more for her than she could expect. She finished brushing Princess, found King Tut, and shoved him into the family room, then left.

That afternoon Auntie said Molly was better. "I hope her folks'll leave her alone for a while. That poor little girl's as weak as a day-old Pomeranian."

"Are you still taking stuff to her?" Shelby asked.

Aunt Rachel nodded. "I make three trips over each day. I take a pitcher of orange juice right after you go to school. At noon I take her some lunch. Then just before anyone gets home, I go gather up the dishes and glasses so they won't know I've been there."

Shelby felt good all over. Auntie was so good. "Did you know you're an angel in disguise?" she asked.

Auntie snorted. "Hardly. But I sure feel sorry for that kid. Let's just hope no one discovers I've been going over there."

But before Shelby finished practicing her flute, she heard loud voices in the entryway. She dropped the instrument into her lap and listened. "This is the last time I'm telling you to keep off my place!" Mr. Lindstrum yelled.

"Try to control yourself, all right?" Uncle said firmly. "Maybe if we watch it, we can talk this over like adults." After a brief silence, Uncle went on. "Your daughter's been seriously ill, Lindstrum. And you didn't even leave any lunch for her. How can you be so upset about Rachel taking over some food?"

"Because you don't know my kid!" the man yelled. After another silence, he cleared his throat and started over. "Everyone gets sick," Shelby heard him say. "But Molly makes everything into a national emergency. If she's sick a day, she turns it into a week. If she stubs her toe, she can't walk for three days."

Shelby dropped a songbook in the silence that followed. It sounded like thunder to her, but the people out in the entryway didn't seem to notice.

"I think you're wrong, Mr. Lindstrum," Aunt Rachel's voice said. "This is the second time I've cared for Molly.

Both times she recovered quicker than I expected. I think you are in serious danger of being neglectful parents."

"I don't care what you consider me!" the man shouted. Then he cursed at Uncle. "Just keep off my place and leave my kid alone. Otherwise, you'll be telling it to the police."

"As a matter of fact, I've been considering doing that again myself." Auntie's voice was so soft that Shelby almost didn't understand what she said. "There are laws about reasonable care of minors. Maybe this time they'd listen to me."

"Just stay off my place!" the man yelled once more. Then there was total silence.

Finally Shelby heard the door close with a small click. Shelby ran out to her uncle and aunt. "How did he find out?" she asked in a hushed voice.

Though her face looked as white as a sheet of paper, Auntie gave Shelby a firm smile. "I didn't get the stuff picked up in time. Don't worry about it, Shelby. It's no big deal."

"Are you going back tomorrow?"

Auntie's smile began to look more normal. And her face colored up a little. "What do you think?" she asked. "That I'm going to let the child starve?"

"Thank you, Auntie," Shelby said. "You're the greatest."

Uncle nodded and put his arm over Auntie's shoulder. "She's the greatest, all right. Maybe she doesn't have sense enough to know when to back off, but she's all right." He shoved his gray hair away from his face and smiled at Shelby.

Shelby finished practicing, then worked with Bunky for a while. "I'm proud of you," she told the dog. "You're starting to stand proud, almost like a real Pom." The dark eyes devoured Shelby with love. And the now-skinny tail gave two wags. "We're going to win if I ever get to show you. I know we will." She put the puppy back into the barricaded kitchen. "You stay there, OK?" The dog shoved the window screen or the card-board aside several times every evening now. Escaping into the living room, she ran like the wind when Shelby tried to catch her. Sometimes Uncle and Auntie had to help.

Aunt Rachel took lunch and orange juice to Molly three more days.

A few days later Shelby asked when they could have the Burtons over.

"We were just talking about that," Auntie said. "How would Saturday night be? We could have a taco salad, play games, and maybe pop some corn later."

"Sounds good. Should I ask LeeAnne?"

Auntie shook her head. "I should do the asking. Give me the number, and I'll do it right now."

Shelby showered while Auntie called. "Mrs. Burton said they'd be delighted to come," Auntie told Shelby when she came out with a pink towel wrapped around her light brown hair. "They're coming next Saturday night. I told them to bring empty stomachs." She started to pick up the newspaper, then looked back at Shelby. "Hey, Bunky's papers came today." She pointed at the corner table, and Shelby picked up the blue envelope.

Shelby tore the envelope open, pulled out the sheet

of paper, and sat down beside Auntie to read it. Bunky's real name, Princess Ebony, looked gorgeous at the top of the page. Then came all her description, followed by her father's name, Ricochet Bullet, and her mother, Misty Rose XXXIV. Shelby pointed at the letters XXXIV. "What does that mean?" she asked.

Auntie looked at the paper. "It means she's the thirty-fourth Pom to be named Misty Rose." She smiled at Shelby. "But your dog is the first to be named Princess Ebony. Aren't you proud of that?"

"Yes." Shelby felt love well up inside her. Then she pointed at the lower half of the paper. "Here's my name," she said. "Shelby Marie Shayne. She's all mine, Auntie." She leaned over and hugged Auntie tight. "Thank you, Auntie. I love you. I love Uncle too. And I love living with you."

Five o'clock Saturday night finally came, in spite of Shelby's fear that it might not. Uncle and Auntie had already met LeeAnne and her mother when they came to see Princess Ebony, and they welcomed their guests warmly. Shelby introduced her aunt and uncle to LeeAnne's twin sisters, Marjie and Katie. After the adults had shaken hands all around and Uncle and Auntie had patted the twins on the head, Aunt Rachel invited them all to the dining room.

"Ah, it looks wonderful," Mr. Burton said as they gathered around the table. He turned to Auntie. "I'm glad I followed your advice."

Auntie looked puzzled.

"Nancy told me that you told us to come with empty stomachs."

Everyone laughed, then, and sat down and bowed

their heads as Uncle thanked God for the meal and for their special guests.

Uncle served the taco salad. "I'll help you with it," he explained, "because it's layered, and we want to be sure you get some of everything."

After Uncle finished serving, the adults began talking. "What kind of work do you do, Mr. Burton?" Uncle asked.

Mr. Burton wiped his mouth with a paper napkin. "Call me Ted," he said. "I teach math at the University of Oregon. My wife Nancy is the head women's basketball coach at the same institution. We both enjoy our work. The place is, shall I say—interesting?" He met his wife's eyes. "How would you describe the U, hon?"

She shook her head. "I don't know—Bohemian? Everyone dresses sort of hippyish." Her mouth curved into a smile. "But it's truly wonderful there. Nearly everyone treats all people alike."

Uncle nodded. "Shelby told how you're having a bad time in your neighborhood."

"Yeah," LeeAnne put in. "They like us so well that they invite us to move all the time."

Everyone ate in silence for a moment.

"I wish I could say that I understand," Auntie said at last, "but I'm not black." She paused as though thinking. "I want you to understand, though. We want to be friends."

LeeAnne's mother reached over and squeezed Auntie's hand. "That means a lot to us," she said. "We appreciate it more than we can say with words."

CHAPTER
10

Bunky Goes Bald

"Everywhere else we've lived, we've been good friends with our neighbors," Ted said. "We've invited them to our place, and they've invited us to theirs. But here we don't feel that friendship. We haven't been invited to anyone's home in the three years we've lived here."

Uncle thought a minute. "You know," he said, "I'd never realized before how much it might mean to our neighbors for us to invite them to our home. We've never invited any neighbors into our home, either."

"I'm surprised," Ted said. "I thought sure it was because we're black. Come to think about it, we've never invited any of our neighbors, either."

"I think everyone's too busy these days to be good neighbors," Uncle said. "It's too bad, but I'm afraid that's the way it is. We're too busy during the week to think about friends. Sometimes we go home with some of our friends for lunch after church or they come home with us, but that's about it."

Nancy wiped her lips on a napkin. "It's sad if neighbors don't socialize anymore," she said, "but in a way it makes me happy. For all we know, one person could be sending all those letters asking us to leave. We may be missing out on some nice people." She smiled at her husband, then laid her fork in her plate. "That was a delicious salad, Rachel. Do you share recipes?"

Auntie looked pretty as she smiled and nodded. "I'm not much of a cook, Nan, but I share what I have."

After dessert Shelby took the Burton girls to her room, where they played Old Maid and Go Fish for the younger girls.

The Burton family left a little before midnight. After everyone had left the kitchen, Bunky reared back on her haunches and jumped, and managed to get her front feet over the top of the window screen. With a push from her back feet, she landed on the other side.

"Oh, oh," Uncle said. "I'm afraid this is the beginning of the end. We won't be able to keep Bunky in jail much longer."

"But she still has accidents," Aunt Rachel said. "Even though she's doing much better."

"Right now I'm taking her to bed," Shelby said. Her eyes felt heavy as she pottied Bunky on the papers in the blue bathroom and stumbled to bed. The puppy never woke in the night anymore, so Shelby knew she'd get a good sleep.

The next morning Bunky let Shelby sleep until almost nine o'clock. After pottying the puppy, Shelby put her into the kitchen enclosure, hoping she'd stay.

And she did—as long as Shelby stayed in the kitchen. But Molly arrived soon after breakfast, and the girls went to Shelby's room. Before Shelby reached her bedroom, the puppy ran up behind her.

"Oh, you sweetie," Shelby said, scooping the dog into her arms. "You want to be with Mommy, don't you?" She put the puppy on the bed.

"What happened to that dog?" Molly asked. "It isn't even cute anymore."

Shelby cuddled the dog a moment before answering. "Oh, yes, she is. She just lost her hair. She'll get some more some day."

"Are you sure? It's really ugly right now. Look at that tail, Shelby. It looks like a worm curled over her back."

Shelby felt her cheeks start to heat. Wait, she couldn't get mad at Molly. Molly's folks treated her so awfully that she just didn't know how to be nice.

"Want to play Chinese checkers?" she asked. "Bunky might sleep on the bed if we play right here."

The girls sat on the carpet beside the bed, and the puppy crept so close to the edge that she lay against Shelby's hair.

Molly's face grew red and her eyes hard when she discovered that Shelby had only one marble left to put into place. Molly's marbles lay all across the board. She lifted her knee and dumped marbles all over the carpet.

Shelby jumped after marbles with both hands. Bunky managed to get off the bed and tried to get her share of the little balls. "Help me, Molly," Shelby cried. "Bunky can't have these things. She'll choke on them."

Molly shrugged. "Who cares? Who'd want such an

ugly thing, anyway?"

Shelby barely kept her tongue under control as she collected the marbles. "You'd better go home, Molly," she said. "I'm going to be practicing my flute and training Bunky. Then I have to do the cats."

Molly's lip came out. "But I wanted to ride bikes."

A wide smile crept over Shelby's face. "That's a great idea. You go for a ride while I do all my chores."

"Hi, girls," Auntie said, coming into the room. "You having a good time?"

"Sure," Shelby said. "So's Bunky. Did you need something?"

"No. I've been thinking about last night. Did you have a good time?"

Shelby gave Molly a quick glance. She had a strong feeling she'd better not say much. She'd seen Molly get jealous before. "Of course. I always have fun." She tried to tell Aunt Rachel with her eyes to hush, but Auntie didn't catch the signal. "But what did you think of the Burtons as a family?"

"The Burtons?" Molly shrieked. "What were you doing with the Burtons? What were you doing last night, Shelby?"

Aunt Rachel threw a shocked look at Shelby.

Shelby reached out a hand and put it on Auntie's arm. "Oh, the Burtons came over. That's all."

"You invited them over, didn't you?" Molly wailed. "You like LeeAnne better than me! You do, Shelby. You've never invited our family over."

Auntie laughed out loud. Then she moved beside Molly and pulled her close. "Molly, sweetie, your family wouldn't come over here. They don't like us much. You knew that, didn't you?"

"They might like you if you'd be nice to them."

Aunt Rachel shook her head. "You must know what our troubles are all about. It's you, Molly. Did you know your dad found out I took lunch and orange juice to you while you were sick a couple of weeks ago? Well, he threatened to call the cops on us."

Molly blinked but showed no other sign of surprise. "I don't care. Shelby likes that black kid better than me. She even likes the dog better than me." Tears oozed from her eyes. "It isn't fair. It just isn't fair!" She got up and ran from the room. A moment later the front door slammed.

"Wow! I really fixed that, didn't I?" Auntie said. "I'm sorry, Shelby. I'm some big help."

"It's all right," Shelby said. "Molly has to do that every once in a while. She's right. It isn't fair that she's stuck in that family. But she can't own me like I own Bunky."

"Well, I'm sorry for opening my mouth. But now that she's gone, I repeat my question. What did you think of the Burtons?"

"They're a wonderful family," Shelby said. "LeeAnne's really nice. She's nice, not only to her friends, but to everyone."

"Should we have them over again?"

"Sure. But I'll bet they'll invite us one of these days." Then another thought popped into Shelby's head. "Hey, Auntie. Remember LeeAnne went to church with me? She really liked it and took part in the lesson. I just sat there like an idiot. Then a few days later she quoted something the lesson said to our schoolteacher. She acted as if it were proven fact."

"I'm glad she liked it, Shelby. Maybe you should invite her again."

"How about this coming weekend? Can she spend the night too?"

"She might like that. Sure, go ahead. Why don't you invite Molly too?"

"OK. But Molly won't be able to come. Not after that fight you had with her dad."

Auntie looked surprised. "That wasn't a fight, Shelby." She stopped a moment. "Well, we did yell at each other a little," she continued. Then she laughed. "Maybe we did have a fight. I can't believe it, kiddo. The James Gobel family in a big fight. Fighting sounds so—uh—common."

Shelby laughed too. "Well, it was for all the best reasons."

That sobered Auntie up. She shook her head. "And that little reason just left, all upset with us." She got up from the bed. "I need to get some washing done. I'm really busy in the office right now." She reached out to give Bunky a couple of pats. "That reminds me. What are we going to do with this little jumper?"

Shelby shook her head. "I don't know. I'll make sure she's either in the kitchen or playpen today, but I don't know what you'll do tomorrow. I'm sorry."

Auntie grinned and tousled Shelby's hair. "It's not your fault, kiddo. But we may as well realize she'll be jumping out of her pen right away too. It isn't any higher than the kitchen barriers."

Shelby dropped back to the bed and held her dog close. "She's right," she whispered into the animal's short black fur. "You're almost uncontrollable." Then she jerked her head back and took a hard look at the dog. She turned it around and looked some more. "Look, Aunt Rachel," she said, pointing. "Bunky's getting some gray hair. See? Right here in what's left of her mane."

Auntie leaned over, parted the dog's fur, and looked long and hard. "I think she is. What do you make of that?"

"It couldn't be from getting old, could it? She's not even grown up yet."

Auntie laughed. "No, it's not old age. Maybe she's not pure Pomeranian after all. She couldn't be part mutt, could she?" A moment later she snapped her fingers. "I know. Let's go talk to Emil about it."

CHAPTER

11

Molly Asks to Spend the Night

Yeah, let's do. His place doesn't smell so great, and the horrible yapping gives Bunky a headache, but I still like to go."

Aunt Rachel hurried out of the bedroom, then stuck her head back in. "Let me put a load of clothes in the washer," she called and took off again.

Molly showed up before they left, so Shelby invited her to go with them to Emil's place. Molly grabbed her nose between her thumb and index finger. "No way. You said it stinks. I'd sooner go to a pig wallow."

Shelby grinned. "OK, but you'll have to find the pig wallow by yourself."

"Can I come over when you get back?"

"Sure. You can help me do the cats."

Molly moaned. "All you ever think about is animals."

"Not true, Molly. But the animals depend on me to care for them."

Auntie came out swinging her car keys on her fingers. "Ready to go?"

Shelby told Molly goodbye and jumped into the front seat beside Aunt Rachel. "Bunky hates that place. But maybe she'll be more used to it this time."

Aunt Rachel grinned. "Just tell her she was born there. Hey, James sent a jar of grape jelly for Emil."

Half an hour later they walked back to the dog pens with the small, quiet man. "I have a new pup," he said. "She's a parti-pom. I call her Bambi." The fluffy black-and-white dog looked a tiny bit bigger than Bunky. And beautiful.

"I'm jealous," Shelby said. "How come she has all that hair?"

Emil ran a hand through Bunky's short fur. "Sometimes they get nearly bald as they go through their awkward stage. Other times you hardly notice."

Shelby thought this must be the perfect time to mention Bunky's new color. "Look, Emil," she said. "My dog's getting some gray hair."

He glanced and shook his head. "She won't get any other color. It's just because she's lost so much hair."

"Maybe she's going to be a parti-pom like Bambi."

Emil smiled, and his eyes had soft lights in them. He shook his head. "I'd like to tell you she's parti-pom," he said. "But she isn't."

Shelby didn't know whether to be relieved or disappointed. That new hair looked kind of pretty, like silver framing her dog's black mane.

Aunt Rachel and Shelby spent some time petting the dogs. Shelby had heard about puppy mills. Those were places where breeders kept their dogs in tiny cages with wire on the bottom. Emil's dogs had nice pens where they could be together with plenty of room for exercise. Shelby liked Emil.

He walked back to the car with them, and Auntie handed Shelby the jar that Uncle had sent. Shelby hesitantly held it out to Emil. "Would you like a jar of grape jelly? It's a little thank-you for our Bunky."

He gladly accepted it, and they drove home.

The next day at school, Shelby waited until Molly was away before inviting LeeAnne to spend Friday night and go to church with her the next day. LeeAnne squealed with joy and hugged Shelby.

Just then, Molly walked into the room. "What's going on?" she asked.

"I'm spending Friday night with Shelby," LeeAnne told her.

"Oh!" Molly glared at Shelby and stomped away.

"If you'd just mentioned you were going to church, she might not have cared," Shelby said, shaking her head. "I don't think she likes church much. She doesn't like Bunky, either. In fact, I don't know why she hangs around me."

LeeAnne laughed. "Because she's like us—the misfits of the world."

Shelby felt as though LeeAnne had punched her in the stomach. "That's not fair," she said. "I mean, you're right. I don't have anyone besides you and Molly. But I'd be your friend anyway." She found her seat for class.

That afternoon Molly came over when Shelby had

finished caring for the cats. "Let's go for a bike ride," she said. "One of these days it's going to snow, and then we won't be able to go anymore."

Shelby laughed. "Snow doesn't last forever, you know." Then she remembered that Molly needed her. "But I'll go for a while."

The girls bundled up in warm parkas and rode down to the lake bed. The water had all been drained from the large lake. "Let's walk on the lake bed," Molly said. "Maybe we can find some arrowheads."

But all they found was mud. Finally Shelby noticed it starting to get dark. "We better get home," she said, "or I'll be in trouble."

As they poked along, Molly brought up the subject of LeeAnne's visit. "You never invite me for overnight," she said.

"Do you think you could come if I asked?"

Molly hesitated. "Maybe. Why don't you ask me tonight?"

All of the many things Shelby still had to do flashed through her mind. "I barely have any free time on week-nights," she said, pedaling even slower. She wobbled but didn't fall. Why couldn't Molly ride faster? "We could have lots more fun this weekend. Besides, there'd be three of us."

Molly swayed a bit, then stood on the pedals to get going a little faster. "Puullease," Molly whined, "let me come tonight. I want to be your best friend. I don't understand how you could like a black girl so much."

"Molly! I don't like LeeAnne better than you. Besides, I never notice her color."

"Let me come tonight, then," Molly whined.

Shelby decided to make Molly ride a little faster, so she sped up a little. A moment later she looked back to see Molly falling farther behind. Shelby kept going. When she came to their driveways, she stopped and waited.

Molly pulled into the Gobel driveway beside Shelby. "That wasn't nice," she said. "You ran away from me because you don't like me anymore."

Shelby laughed. "You're silly, Molly. I'll ask Aunt Rachel if you can spend the night tonight, but your dad won't let you."

Molly brightened. "Goody. Let's go ask."

Shelby shook her head. "I'm going to ask, Molly. You're going home. If Aunt Rachel says OK, I'll call you."

Molly didn't like that much, but she went. "You better call me," she yelled as she pedaled across the road to her own place.

"Sure, go call her," Auntie said after Shelby explained her problem.

"Cross your fingers she can't come," Shelby said. "I have a lot to do."

"I'm not crossing my fingers," Aunt Rachel said. "You can skip some of your stuff. It would be a good deed for you to help Molly feel wanted."

Shelby shuddered as she dialed the number. Who would answer the phone, and what would they say?

"Hello," a gruff voice growled into her ear.

She swallowed twice. "Hello, Mr. Lindstrum. May I speak to Molly?"

"What do you want?"

Should she tell him or hold out to talk to Molly?

Talking to Molly won out. "I need to speak to her about something important—please?"

The silence lasted so long Shelby thought he'd hung up on her. "Make it quick. I'm expecting a call." He dropped the phone on the table.

"Hello?" Molly's small voice asked a moment later.

"Hi, Molly. It's me. Auntie said you can come. How about you?"

"I'll have to ask. Then I'll call you back, OK?"

Shelby waited by the phone for ten minutes, then went to her bedroom to practice her flute. Auntie or Uncle would get the phone. Then she got into her music and forgot about Molly. When she finished, she remembered.

"Did the phone ring for me?" she asked Auntie in the kitchen.

Aunt Rachel shook her head. "It didn't ring for anyone. Who were you expecting, Molly?"

"Yes, she was going to call about spending the night." She looked at the clock and grinned. "I guess this means No."

Just then, the phone rang, and Shelby jumped to answer it. But it still wasn't Molly. LeeAnne said she could spend Friday night and Sabbath with Shelby. Molly didn't call.

The next morning Shelby couldn't wait to talk to Molly. "What happened last night?" she asked as the girls walked to the bus.

Molly flipped her head as if the question were foolish. "He didn't want me to go," she said. "Big deal!"

"I thought you were going to call back and tell me."

"He wouldn't let me. But I guess you figured it out."

"Sure. About ten o'clock. What about Friday night?"
Molly shrugged. "I don't know."

"Well, you're invited."

They ran across the road as the bus approached.

The days sped by, with Shelby practicing her music, training her dog, and caring for the cats. Shane Anderson came over and played with Bunky once in a while.

Bunky kept getting out of the kitchen barriers. Everyone put her back, and no one got impatient with the tiny puppy.

Friday afternoon, Jon met Shelby when she raced into the band room. "Hey, did you hear?" he asked.

He looked so sincere that Shelby fell for it. "No, what?"

"No need to repeat it if you didn't hear the first time."

"What are you talking about?" she asked, thoroughly confused.

"And if you can't hear, you may as well drop out of band. I never heard of a deaf musician."

Shelby gave a disgusted sigh and headed for her chair.

LeeAnne, Molly, and Shelby talked as they waited for the buses that afternoon. "Have you asked if you can come?" Shelby asked Molly.

"No, and I'm not going to. I won't mess up your wonderful time."

"We want you, Molly," LeeAnne said. "We're making chocolate popcorn."

"And we're sleeping with Bunky," Shelby said with a twinkle. "I know you'll like that!"

CHAPTER

12

A Missing Flute

I said I'm not coming," Molly said. "So you two can tell each other how glad you are." The buses came, and Shelby and Molly climbed onto theirs.

Later in the afternoon Aunt Rachel helped Shelby and LeeAnne make chocolate popcorn, which they ate while playing Bible games.

LeeAnne joined in praying for Jon Greenflower during worship. She said it would be hard to hate someone you were praying for.

The next morning Shelby could tell that LeeAnne enjoyed Sabbath School. Shelby felt relieved when the kids acted as though they were all the same color. The last time LeeAnne had visited, Shelby hadn't given it a thought. But last time she didn't know how mean some people treat blacks. LeeAnne's hand shot up as often as anyone's, and though she made some mistakes, it didn't seem to bother her. She kept on trying. Shelby didn't answer at all.

Late in the afternoon the phone rang, and Auntie answered it. After hanging up, Auntie said that Nancy Burton had invited the Gobel family over for a light snack and games that evening.

"I told you they'd ask," Shelby whispered to Auntie.

Bunky cried when Shelby locked her in the bathroom before they left. "I'm sorry," Shelby said. "I don't like to cage you up, but you do bad things. When you get housetrained, you can run loose."

The Burtons served a large bowl of fruit salad, together with ice cream, and cookies. Then the kids and adults stayed together and played a game that the Burtons had made up—a long, complicated game that took the whole evening. Each person had a list of things to do and find. Shelby couldn't remember ever having had more fun.

"Hey, it's snowing," Uncle said when they opened the door to go home.

"Good. We haven't had any snow since I came," Shelby said. "We had lots of snow every year in New York."

Uncle drove slowly and carefully. Though no snow had accumulated on the ground, the swirling white flakes made visibility almost zero. Uncle leaned forward and gripped the steering wheel tightly.

By Monday morning eight inches of the sparkling stuff canceled school for the day. Wearing boots, Shelby slowly made her way to the Stratton place to care for the cats. When she had finished, she struggled home again.

"Let's take a bike ride," she called across the road to Molly.

"Are you crazy or what?" Molly yelled back.

Shelby gave up for then and did all the things she did every day. When she had finished, her eyes turned outside to the beautiful snowy scene.

Then her bike popped back into her mind. She got it and managed to ride it slowly down the driveway, sliding in every direction. Then she rode down the road about halfway to Ellmaker Road. Hard work! She panted so hard as she put her bike back into the garage that she reminded herself of Molly.

After reading a book for an hour, her eyes strayed again to the snow-covered world outside. Bunky had never seen snow. She might as well take her out.

Shelby put on her heavy parka once more, then her boots, mittens, and bulky stocking cap. Then she remembered Bunky in her playpen upstairs. "Auntie," she called. "I forgot Bunky. Could you bring her down?"

A few minutes later Aunt Rachel plopped the puppy into Shelby's arms. "She isn't going to like the snow much," she said. "Watch her closely and bring her in when she starts to get cold."

Shelby looked into Bunky's soft brown eyes. "Here I am, all dressed for the cold," she told the tiny dog, "and you're almost naked. You need a coat. I should ask Auntie to teach me how to knit you one." The small dog's head tipped from side to side as she tried to understand Shelby.

"Hey, Shayne," Shane Anderson's voice called out as he came around the house. "What're you trying to do to that innocent little dog?"

Shelby felt glad to see Shane. He always said he came to see Bunky, but Shelby enjoyed his company a lot. His kindness almost made up for Jon's meanness.

"Just seeing how she likes the snow," Shelby replied.

Shelby set the puppy down in the white stuff, and immediately Bunky sank in over her head. Shelby laughed. "Doesn't take much to swamp you, does it?"

Bunky gave several hard leaps and managed to travel slowly across the backyard. As she got her bearings in the confusing white world, the little dog's leaps all brought her nearer to the house. When she reached the back door, she stood shivering, yelping to go in.

Shelby ran lightly across the snow, scooped up the puppy, and took her inside. "You're not even as brave as I expected," she told the small animal. Grabbing a large, soft bath towel from the downstairs shower, she rubbed Bunky until her short fur felt dry and fluffy again.

Shane stayed long enough to play with Bunky awhile and to watch her play with the little white toy dog he'd given her when she was so tiny. He always asked Shelby to get the toy so he could see how much Bunky had grown. The puppy looked huge beside the toy that had once been her size.

"How much does Bunky weigh now?" he asked.

"About five pounds," Shelby said. She shook her head. "She seems so tiny now that I can hardly believe she weighed one pound three months ago."

School started again the next day, and Shelby and Molly had a hard time walking to meet the bus. A light snow was falling.

"I don't know why they don't plow out Marina Drive," Molly grumbled.

Shelby laughed. "Because it's just a little road. They're busy doing the main roads so people can get to work." She held out her hand, catching the slowly falling flakes on her glove. "Just think how pretty it is."

They barely made it to the stop before the bus lumbered to a halt, its tire chains jangling. "Stomp the snow off," the driver growled.

Shelby stomped her feet as she climbed the steps into the warm bus.

A little while later the big yellow vehicle pulled into the schoolyard and stopped with a swish of its brakes. Shelby ran down the steps onto the already-shoveled sidewalk. Her foot slipped a little, so she took off running. "Come on, Molly," she yelled, "we can skate." Then she looked back to see how Molly was doing.

Molly didn't run or slide. She inched carefully along the icy sidewalk. "You'd better be careful," she called. "If you fall, you may break a leg."

"Oh, come on, Molly." Shelby took another run and slid six feet before a giant snowball hit her on the side of the head. She saw some bright flashes and tumbled to the sidewalk. Another snowball hit her hard on the arm as she went down, but she barely felt it.

The next thing she knew, Molly was shaking her coat collar. "Shelby, get up."

Shelby looked at the ring of kids surrounding her. Feeling too fuzzy to be embarrassed, she tried to get her feet under her. Molly took her arm and helped. About the time Shelby began to feel steady on her feet, a hard snowball hit Molly on the back of the head. Her knees buckled, and Shelby held her up.

"What's going on here?" a deep voice asked. "Throwing snowballs is one thing, but trying to hurt people is something else." Shelby recognized the voice as belonging to Mr. Wesley, one of the math teachers. She whirled to see him looking around. "Who threw these snowballs?" he called. No one answered.

"I'm not very happy about this," he said sternly. "If this happens again, I'll do whatever it takes to find the guilty person. Whoever did it should take a hard look at himself. Only a sick person likes to hurt others."

The laughing group quieted until Shelby almost heard the snow falling. She helped Molly into the school, then ran to her first class.

That afternoon Shelby hurried to band, glad that school would soon be out. She wanted to play in the snow some more. Maybe Sandy had an old sled in the garage. She and Molly could slide down the bank of the lawn.

Busy thinking about the snow, she forgot to notice that Jon didn't give her a bad time about being an orphan—or anything else. Band went well. Shelby could play her flute better than anyone else. Mrs. Beecher asked her to help a girl who couldn't figure out the fingering for a hard note. Showing the girl where to put her fingers, Shelby silently thanked Sandy for helping her so much last summer.

When school dismissed, all the kids started throwing snowballs at each other again. Shelby threw her share of the soft and harmless balls. "Let's make a snowman when we get home," she yelled at Molly.

"OK," Molly called back. "Hey, the buses are loading." Shelby dropped her half-formed snowball and ran back to the school porch for her book bag. She barely made it onto the bus before the door closed. Relaxing quietly, she watched the few lazy snowflakes still falling. The warmth of the bus and the beauty of the snow outside made Shelby feel cozy and comfortable—and lazy. But before she knew it, she found herself out in the snowy world again.

"I'm cold," Molly grumbled as they walked home. "I'd like snow better if it wasn't so cold." As soon as she realized what she'd said, she looked at Shelby, and both girls laughed.

"I like it just the way it is," Shelby said. "Want to find something to slide on when I finish the cats?"

"Maybe. If the wicked witch doesn't get home first."

"I'll hurry." Shelby walked in car tracks where the snow wasn't so deep and cut her time with the cats a few minutes so they'd be sure to have time.

"Hi, Auntie," she called as she stepped inside the house. "Can I go sliding with Molly?"

"Come on in," her aunt called from the office.

Shelby hurried down the hall and lifted Bunky from her playpen. The little dog went nearly crazy greeting Shelby. "Is there a sled or anything around here that I could use?" Shelby asked, wiping Bunky's kisses from her face.

Aunt Rachel stood up and stretched her arms. "Sandy got a plastic sled a few years ago. I think it's hanging on the garage wall. Let's go look."

A few minutes later Shelby carried a yellow sled with red trim out to the road. Should she go after Molly? What if her stepmother had come while she did the cats? Oh, well, she didn't see any fresh tracks in the snow. She started toward the house, then chickened out and trotted back home. She'd call.

"Hello!" a stern voice said over the phone a few minutes later. Shelby jumped and almost hung up the phone, but she managed to stay on the line. "Hello, Mrs. Lindstrum, may I speak to Molly, please?"

"You've been with her all day at school. What's with you kids anyway?" She banged the telephone down. Shelby sat down, shaking her head. How did people get so mean, anyway?

After resting and collecting her thoughts for a few moments, she decided she'd take Bunky out for a little while. She dressed the puppy in two pairs of fuzzy pajamas, put on her own parka, hood, and boots, then ran out the door.

"How'd you like to slide with me?" she asked the puppy.

She carried the sled and dog to the edge of the bank at the front of the lawn. Then she sat down on the sled with Bunky securely in her arms and pushed off. The ten-foot bank hardly gave her time to get started, but she carried it to the top a few times and slid down. Bunky huddled close to Shelby.

"I don't think you enjoy sledding very much," Shelby finally told her puppy. "Let's put the sled away and go in, OK?"

After cleaning Bunky's feet and fur, she put the dog on her bed and picked up her book bag. Might as well practice awhile before supper. Opening the big blue bag, she dumped it on the carpet. Books, papers, a scarf, and her Walkman tumbled out. But where was the flute? She lifted the limp book bag and peered inside. It was empty!

Her heart began racing. Could she have left her flute in the band room? She shook her head and wiped her sweating upper lip. She remembered snapping the flute case closed and fitting it into the bag beside her books.

Snatching Bunky into her arms, she headed downstairs.

"Auntie, I can't find my flute!"

CHAPTER

13

The Flute Is Stolen

Uncle looked up and grinned. "Hey, it isn't that serious," he said. "Take another look around your room. It'll turn up." He pulled up the corners of Shelby's mouth with his fingers. "That flute means a lot to you, doesn't it?"

"Yes, and I remember putting the flute in the book bag," she said. "Could I have lost it on the way home?"

Auntie had wrapped her arms around Shelby by this time. "When you shut that bag, it's shut. Remember your big hurry to go sledding? I'll bet you took it out and put it somewhere. Think, kiddo. Try to remember."

Shelby thought. She'd run to her room, dropped the bag on the floor, and gone back out. Then another picture flashed into her mind. She turned teary eyes back to Aunt Rachel. "Oh, no! I left my bag on the porch at school while we waited for the bus. We threw snowballs, and I didn't want my stuff to get wet."

"Call the school," Uncle said. "Someone probably put it inside."

"No, Uncle. I got the bag when the bus came. But the flute's not in it!"

"So how did the flute get out of the bag?" Uncle asked.

"Someone stole it!" Auntie spit the words from her mouth as though they tasted bad.

Suddenly Shelby couldn't catch her breath. The lump in her throat grew larger, and she felt dizzy. She sat down on the carpet.

Auntie dropped down beside Shelby and pulled her into her arms. "Don't worry, Shelby, we'll get it back." She patted Shelby for a moment. "Or I'll tear that school apart trying," she added.

Uncle smiled at Auntie. "You'd better start tonight," he said. "The trail will be cold by tomorrow."

Auntie got up and pulled Shelby up beside her. "I'll call the principal," she said. She dialed the number and talked a few minutes. "They'll check it out tomorrow," she said after hanging up the phone. She glanced at Shelby, who sat with Bunky in her lap. "He thinks Shelby left it in the band room."

Shelby shook her head. "I didn't. I remember moving a book to make a nest for the flute in the bag." She paused. "Auntie's right. Someone took my flute." Suddenly Shelby knew who did it! Jon. No one else would be so mean. "And I know who did it," she said. "The guy who always picks on me for being an orphan. And on LeeAnne for being black. I hate Jonathan Greenflower! I hate him so much."

Uncle shook his head. "We don't *know* that he took the flute. Teasing girls and stealing flutes are not the same thing. And you don't hate anyone, remember?"

Tears filled Shelby's eyes again. "You just don't know him, Uncle. He's rotten clear through."

Uncle shook his head again. "You absolutely must let the school investigate this thing, Shelby. Don't you say anything to the boy? Hear?"

Shelby shrugged. "I guess."

"Come on, let's fix dinner," Auntie said.

They all helped make the meal, but Shelby had to force her food down. Afterward she tried to do some math, and she sat while Uncle and Auntie watched "Full House," but she couldn't follow the story line. Would she have to drop band? That was her very favorite subject. For sure, Uncle James and Aunt Rachel would never trust her with anything again.

After Bible study they all prayed for the return of the flute. Auntie and Uncle prayed for Jon, but Shelby couldn't. Afterward she told them how sorry she was for being careless and asked them to forgive her.

"You weren't careless," Aunt Rachel said. "You put the book bag on the porch to keep it dry. That's more than I'd have done when I was a kid." She gave Shelby a small whack on the rear. "Now go get a good sleep."

But Shelby couldn't fall asleep. She knew positively that Jon had taken her flute just to be mean. And she bet he threw the snowballs that hurt her and Molly. She'd never known anyone so mean, and she truly did hate him. *Forgive me, Jesus, but I do hate him. I can't help it.*

Still she couldn't fall asleep. Finally she asked God to help her know if Jonathan Greenflower took her flute.

As she waited for an answer, the Lord's Prayer flitted through her mind: "Forgive my sins as I forgive those who sin against me." She bolted upright in bed. She could never forgive Jon for stealing her flute! Never!

She lay back down. She didn't know why that scripture came to her right then, but she did know that Jon had taken her flute, and she'd make him pay.

The next morning the sun shone brightly on the still-white snow. It made Shelby feel better. When she met Molly in the road, she forgot all about the sledding incident. Or rather, the not-sledding. She remembered how mean Molly's stepmother had been, but it seemed long ago and not very important.

"I suppose you had more fun sledding without me," Molly grumbled, scuffing through the snow. "I could tell you didn't want me to go anyway."

Shelby felt like telling Molly what a jerk she was. Striding a few steps before answering, she remembered Molly's unloving home. She'd better be nice to her. "Molly," she said patiently, "do you remember who asked you to go sledding?" She pointed a gloved finger at her chest. "I wouldn't have asked you to go if I didn't want you. In fact, without you, it wasn't even fun. I went down the bank only a few times."

They walked in silence a few minutes.

"Hey, someone stole my flute yesterday," Shelby told her grumpy friend.

Molly stopped walking, then shook her head and went on. "You're kidding me," she said.

"No, I'm not," Shelby insisted. "Remember when we threw snowballs after school? Someone stole it out of my book bag then."

"Wow. Did your uncle and aunt kill you?"

Until that moment, Shelby hadn't thought about how kind they'd been. "No, they were really nice. They felt sorry for me and promised to help me get it back."

When they got to school, Shelby found a message to report to the principal's office right away. The secretary waved her on into the inner office. "He's waiting for you," she said kindly.

Shelby tiptoed back and eased the door open. "Don't act like a scared mouse," Mr. Brickner's deep voice said. "Open the door and come in." Shelby went in and sat in the blue plastic chair the principal indicated. "Did you check the band room for your flute?" he asked. "I went through it carefully," he continued, not giving her a chance to answer. "I found nothing, of course, and Mrs. Beecher saw you put the flute into a blue book bag. Did you get home with the bag?"

Shelby nodded. She didn't know why the little round, bald-headed man made her so nervous. He looked like someone who should be driving a school bus. "Everything was in it except the flute. Someone stole it, Mr. Brickner." She explained to him how she'd put the blue bag on the porch while waiting for the bus.

"Well, we'll be checking into that possibility," he said kindly. "Now you go on back to class and try to forget all about it. Hopefully we'll have it back before your band period."

A few minutes later Shelby slid into her seat, trying hard to be invisible, but when she raised her eyes, they met Jonathan Greenflower's bright blue ones. He raised his eyebrows and grinned as if they shared a secret. Dropping her eyes, she refused to look at him again.

CHAPTER

14

Shelby Hurts Jon

About an hour later a tall girl brought in a notice from the office. Mrs. Huntley put down her book and read it to the class. It told about a missing flute and asked the prankster to please take the instrument to the office. It also asked anyone who knew who took it to report it. It ended with a statement about the integrity of the school and the hope of keeping it that way.

Shelby couldn't help peeking through her hair at Jon. Just as she'd expected, she caught him looking at her. His grin assured her that he knew whose flute had been taken and who did it. Him! She wanted more than anything to go tell Mr. Brickner about Jon. But she'd promised Uncle. Maybe Uncle would change his mind tonight.

The flute hadn't been returned by band period, so

Shelby went to study hall. But a few minutes later Jon came to tell her that Mrs. Beecher wanted her to help one of the other flute players.

Shelby couldn't handle his friendliness as they walked down the deserted hall to the band room. "I know you took my flute," she told him. "You've done everything you could think of to convince me."

He looked baffled. "What would I want with a flute?"

"To torment me, of course. I don't know why you hate me, but you do. I don't know why you're such a jerk, either."

He laughed loudly. "So you think I have your flute, huh? What are you going to do about it?"

"Give it to me, Jon. I don't want to miss band for even one day."

He laughed again. "Why don't you make me? If you really think I have the silly thing, why don't you make me give it back?"

"You give it to me right now, or you'll wish you had."

He stopped and faced her in the wide, deserted hall, still smiling. "I haven't even admitted I took the piece of junk. Haven't you heard that a person is innocent until someone proves he's guilty?"

Shelby put her hands on her hips. "Did you take my flute, Jonathan Greenflower?"

"Know what the fifth amendment is?" he asked. "It means you don't have to answer questions about yourself that might make you look guilty. Well, I'm sorry, but I have to take the fifth."

Shelby felt her neck and face burn. The muscles in her hands tightened until she felt her hands form fists. Worse yet, tears threatened to pour into her eyes.

"You're a real jerk," she said. "Did you hear Mr. Wesley say that whoever likes to hurt people is sick? Well, Jonathan Greenflower, you're sick. You're the meanest and sickest person I've ever known."

He didn't say a word. He just grabbed her hand and started spinning her around him. She tripped all over the floor trying to keep her balance as he spun her around. After a couple of rounds, she managed to stop and stand steadily on her feet. She stomped on both of Jonathan's feet as hard as she could, then, using every bit of her strength she gave him a gigantic push. To her surprise, he fell to the floor with a crash. It sounded super loud and echoed up and down the empty hall. She turned to go on to the band room but had taken only a few steps when she heard him crying. Jonathan Greenflower crying? Then he began sobbing loudly. She went right on to the band room without even looking back.

"Well," Mrs. Beecher said with a smile. "At last. I thought you'd never come. I guess you haven't heard anything."

Shelby shook her head and sank into her chair. Mrs. Beecher asked her to help two girls while they practiced. After class Mrs. Beecher asked Shelby to stay behind. "Would you like to use a school instrument until you find yours?" she asked. "It isn't being used."

"Oh, yes, Mrs. Beecher. If you can trust me with a school instrument."

The teacher patted her shoulder. "Of course, I trust you."

Shelby hurried to the bus.

"You'll never guess what I did today," Shelby said to

her plump little friend as they plowed through the snow down Marina Drive.

"I probably won't," Molly said. "Got your flute back, maybe?"

Shelby shook her head. "Nope. I got into a fight with Jon Greenflower."

Molly looked disappointed. "So what else is new? You always do that."

Shelby grinned. Still she felt awful. "No, Molly," she explained, "I got into a real fight with him. I won too. The last I heard from him, he lay on the hall floor, crying his beautiful blue eyes out."

Molly's eyes lighted up, and she smiled. The smile reminded Shelby that she hadn't seen Molly smile much lately. "All right!" Molly said. "Maybe he'll pick on someone his own size now." Her mouth opened. "Oops," she said. "I didn't mean you're big, Shelby. Well, you *are* big, but . . ."

Shelby laughed and took Molly's hand. "Better stop while you're ahead, Molly. I know I'm big, and I don't mind. But what do you think about Jon?"

"I hope he's still on the floor crying when we get to school tomorrow."

When Shelby got home, she told Uncle James and Aunt Rachel about the incident. "I can't believe I did it," she said when she finished.

"I'm sorry you did," Uncle said, "but I understand. The kid pushed you over the edge. Well, we'll just wait and see what happens."

The phone rang that night, and Uncle answered. "Yes, I'm James Gobel. May I help you?" he asked, raising his eyebrows at Shelby. Pause. "Yes, she lives here." Pause. "Look, Mr. Greenflower, I'm not discussing this with you tonight. Meet me tomorrow at school, and Mr. Brickner can mediate." Pause. Uncle James shook his head sadly. "Well, there may be a surprise or two in this for you too, Greenflower. It's just possible that you haven't heard the whole story." After another long pause, he slowly replaced the receiver. "He gave me a vivid picture of what he thinks of me and hung up," Uncle said.

Aunt Rachel jumped from her seat and clung to Uncle's arm. "What's wrong?" she asked.

"It seems that his poor little boy has a broken bone or two in his foot," Uncle James said.

Aunt Rachel laughed. She actually laughed! "Way to go, kiddo," she said. "If anyone ever deserved a broken foot, that kid did."

Uncle held out a hand. "That's not our Lord's way, Rachel. How many times did He say we should forgive?"

Shelby knew the answer to that, but she'd never felt the pinch of it before. "It says seventy times seven," she said. "But I think Jon's passed the four hundred and ninety mark." She nodded thoughtfully. "I really do."

Uncle messed up her hair. "You don't really believe He meant that literally? That you don't have to forgive the four hundred and ninety-first offense, do you?"

She shook her head. "I guess not. But it's going to be hard to forgive all the things he's done to me and my friends. What happens now, Uncle?"

The phone rang again before he answered. He picked it up and spoke. Then he gave Shelby a tight grin. "Yes, this is James Gobel. What can I do for you,

Mr. Brickner?" Pause. "Did you believe the man's story? Or are you familiar with that kid?" Pause. "Good. Of course, we'll be there. We're as eager to get this straightened out as you are. Thanks for calling."

He hung up the phone and turned to Shelby again. "Greenflower's a busy little man tonight," he said. "That was your principal calling us to a meeting in the morning. I guess your bullying that innocent kid finally caught up with you, Shelby." He messed up Shelby's hair and got up. "Let's have worship. And it would be good if you could ask to be forgiven for reacting to the boy, Shelby." Shelby did but told God He knew all the things Jon had done to her. Uncle told them good night and hurried to his bedroom.

Aunt Rachel moved to the couch beside Shelby. "Don't look so sad," she said. "When we get this kid in his place, your life will be a whole lot better."

Shelby took Bunky to her paper in the bathroom. "Hey," she said to the tiny dog, "you haven't been messing up the house lately. Maybe you're growing up at last." Shelby and Bunky climbed into bed. The tiny black ball of fur settled close to her and fell asleep. Shelby didn't fare so well. She awakened often through the night. Each time, she told her heavenly Father how much she loved Him and how much she wanted to do His will. Then each time she confessed how she didn't feel all that sorry for hurting Jon Greenflower.

The next morning Shelby told Molly all the new developments. "I hope he gets kicked out of school," Molly said, puffing to keep up. "Do you think I could go to that meeting with you?"

Shelby kept hurrying down the road toward the bus

stop. She laughed at Molly's suggestion. "I doubt it," she said. "His parents will be there, and so will Aunt Rachel and Uncle James. But thanks for the moral support anyway."

Shelby had barely stepped into her home room when Mrs. Huntley informed her that the principal wanted her in his office.

"Go on in, hon," the principal's secretary told her with a smile.

But Mr. Brickner didn't smile when Shelby stepped into his office. "Thanks for coming," he said, glancing up from the paper before him. He pushed the paper to the edge of his desk and met her eyes. Finally he smiled, and his eyes looked calm and kind. "I thought it only fair for me to hear your side of this story before everyone arrives," he said. "Mr. Greenflower painted a rather ugly little picture of your confrontation with his son." He pointed to a chair at the corner of his desk, and Shelby sat down. She took a deep breath but didn't say anything. He nodded at her. "Just tell me what happened yesterday, all right?"

What should she tell him? A couple of days ago, Uncle had said she shouldn't accuse Jon of taking her flute, but how could she tell about their fight without saying so? If she didn't tell the exact truth, she'd surely get mixed up. She had to tell it all. She started to speak but felt something coating her throat. She cleared it and tried again. "What did he tell you, Mr. Brickner?"

The principal smiled but shook his head. "I'm waiting for your version. I'm sure you've heard the old cliche, 'There are two sides to every story.' Well, I'm waiting to hear the flip side of the record."

Shelby thought a moment. "Well, Jon came to tell me Mrs. Beecher wanted me in the band room. On the way he started picking on me about my missing flute." She stopped and looked into Mr. Brickner's eyes again. "He took it, you know."

The principal jerked upright. "No, I certainly didn't know. Why didn't you tell me that in the beginning?"

Shelby shrunk into the seat a little. "Because I don't know for really sure. But I do know he did it."

The man nodded. "I see. All right, go on with your story, Shelby."

"I told him I knew he took the flute, and he asked me what I was going to do about it. I yelled at him to bring it back, or he'd be sorry. Then he grabbed my hand and started whirling me."

"Right there in the hall?"

"Yes. No one was around, though. Well, finally I got my feet under me enough to stomp on his feet. Both of them, and really hard. Then I shoved him down and ran to the band room."

The principal met Shelby's gaze a moment, then smiled. "I believe you, Shelby, and thank you for telling me. But why do you think Jon took your flute? What would he want with it?"

Shelby clasped her hands, then unclasped them. "He didn't want it. But for some reason he hates me. He does every nasty thing he can to me and says awful things to me too. That's how I know he took it."

Mr. Brickner shook his head. "That's not even circumstantial evidence, Shelby. Just because he's mean doesn't prove he's a thief. You shouldn't have accused him of stealing it."

CHAPTER

15

Shelby Is Vindicated

Shelby felt as if her principal had promised her a prize, then jerked it away. When he told her he believed her, she'd thought everything would be all right. But now he was mad at her for accusing Jon of stealing the flute. Come to think about it, Uncle told her not to do that.

"I'm sorry, Mr. Brickner," she said in a tiny voice. "Uncle James told me not to do that too, but I did and . . ." Suddenly tears streamed from her eyes. Mr. Brickner handed her several tissues. She scrubbed her eyes and swallowed a few times. ". . . and I can't take it back," she managed to finish.

"It's all right," the man said. "We'll just go . . ."

The intercom came to life at that moment. "Sorry to interrupt, Mr. Brickner," his secretary said, "but Mr. and Mrs. Greenflower are here with Jon. Mr. and Mrs.

Gobel are here too."

Mr. Brickner got up from his chair and helped Shelby dry her face. "It's all right," he said. "Just relax, and it'll be all over in a little while." He turned back to the intercom. "We're ready now. Send them in, please."

Suddenly the room seemed wall to wall with people. Uncle James and Aunt Rachel sat on a couch against the wall. Uncle beckoned for Shelby to sit between them, which she gladly did.

Jonathan followed his parents in. He used crutches and did such a bad job of handling them that Shelby felt sorry for him. When they reached the chairs, his mother took his crutches and helped him into the seat.

"So that's the Jezebel who did it!" Mr. Greenflower said. "She looks big enough to take on a guy, all right. I'd hate for her to . . ."

"All right," Mr. Brickner interrupted, "let's get started. Jonathan, why don't you tell us exactly how you got hurt."

Jon flashed Shelby a desperate look, then turned to the principal. "She just stomped on my feet with all her might and pushed me down. I didn't realize something like that could break bones, but here I am."

The principal nodded his head. "Do you have any idea *why* she'd do such a mean thing? Is she always like that?"

"No," Jon said, shaking his head. "She's usually really nice."

"Nice girls don't act like that," Jon's dad said.

Mr. Brickner ignored Mr. Greenflower. "Did you do or say anything to cause her actions?"

"Of course, he didn't," Mrs. Greenflower said. "What

could he have done to cause her to break his foot?"

Mr. Brickner ignored Jon's mother. He leaned toward Jon across his desk. "Why don't you try to remember, Jon. Can you think of anything you might have done?"

Jon hesitated for a long time, then shook his head. "I just went after her for Mrs. Beecher." He stopped a moment, then slapped his forehead. "She accused me of stealing her flute," he said. "She got really mad about that."

Jon's parents jerked to attention at Jon's words. "What's that about stealing a flute?" his dad yelled. Then he glared at Uncle James. "I'll sue you for every cent you own."

The principal ignored the man. "Did you steal the flute?" he asked Jon.

Jon's face flushed, starting at the neck and rising to his hair. "Wh-wh-what would I want with a flute?" he finally managed to ask.

Mr. Brickner smiled. Even his eyes smiled. "I didn't ask if you needed a flute, Jon," he said quietly. "I'll repeat the question. Did you *take* Shelby's flute?"

Jon scratched his head. He cracked three knuckles. He glanced at Shelby twice. Then he shook his head. "No," he whispered.

Shelby jumped to her feet. "He did too!" she yelled. "You can tell he's guilty just by watching him. He has it hidden someplace, just to be mean."

"Siddown, young lady," Mr. Greenflower yelled. "Did you see him take your flute?"

Shelby sat down. She looked at the floor. She could feel the man's eyes drilling into her. She shook her head.

"Can you control yourself, Shelby?" the principal asked.

"Of course she can't," Mrs. Greenflower said sarcastically. "She's just getting ready to take on someone else. I'm telling you, Mr. Brickner, you'd better get her out of this school, or I'm calling your superintendent."

Mr. Brickner stood up. "The meeting's over," he said quietly. He stepped over and opened the door. "Goodbye, Mr. and Mrs. Greenflower. Jon, you may go to your class."

"What you going to do with that wild kid?" Jon's dad asked as he walked toward the open door.

"I'll handle this," Mr. Brickner said. After they left, he shut the door behind them and turned back to Shelby. He gave a loud sigh. "You did it again, Shelby," he said. "Why?"

"I couldn't help it," she said. "And don't tell me you think he's innocent."

The man shook his head. "I don't know what to think. The fight in the hall seems to be your word against his. And he came away with serious injuries. I'm giving you Inner-School-Suspension for a week. That means you'll come to school but won't attend classes. You'll stay in study hall. At the end of the week, we'll have another look at this thing, and your attitude."

Uncle stood to his feet. "That's not fair to Shelby," he said. "It would take an hour to tell you all the things that kid has said and done to Shelby and other kids too."

The principal glanced at his watch. "Unfortunately I don't have an hour," he said. "And the boy would deny it." Then he turned to Shelby. "You may go to study hall now, Shelby. If you can't find anything to do there, you can help me here in my office. Only if you'd like to."

Uncle held his hand out to Mr. Brickner. "I don't envy you your job, sir. But our girl doesn't lie. She's kind and caring. And I guarantee she put up with more before she lost her temper than either you or I would have."

The principal shook Uncle's hand. "I'm glad you have confidence in your daughter. Every parent should feel that way about his child. I'm sure you noticed Jon Greenflower's parents do too." He shook his head. "Sorry about this whole thing, folks, but I have an appointment that began about five minutes ago." He rushed off down the hall.

Uncle and Auntie got ready to leave. " 'Bye 'bye, kiddo," Aunt Rachel said. "This isn't the end, you know."

Shelby ambled toward the room she'd been suspended to. She just hoped she wouldn't see Jon Greenflower again that day. The way she felt, she might hurt him even worse than she had before.

She studied ahead in all of her subjects that day. Not far enough, though. She'd be out of class for a whole week.

About the middle of the afternoon a bunch of boys came in, laughing and shoving. One of the boys turned to Jon Greenflower. "What kind of flute is it?"

"I dunno, but I'll sell it cheap."

Just then, the bell rang, and everyone quieted down. The teacher took her place in front of the room. "I've been asked to read an announcement at the beginning of each period," she said. "Flute left on south school porch missing since yesterday. If you know anything about this instrument, please report it to someone. The instrument is badly needed."

"Hey," one of the boys said. "Find out who lost the flute and sell yours to her or him."

"Shut up!" Jon whispered loudly.

"Do you boys know something about this?" the teacher asked.

"No!" Jon snapped.

"But he has a flute to sell," the first boy said. "If that person don't find his or hers, send them to Jon."

Shelby wanted to jump up and shout that Jon had *her* flute, but she'd messed up twice already. She'd better keep quiet and tell Uncle James. She didn't know the other boy, but she took a long look at him from the back. She had to find out who he was.

When the bell rang, the kids got up to leave. Shelby sat still and watched the boy turn around and walk toward the door. She'd seen him around but didn't know his name.

She walked up to the teacher. "May I please go help Mr. Brickner? He said I could if I got bored."

The teacher smiled and told her to go.

"Are you applying for work?" the principal asked when Shelby walked into his office.

She nodded. "I got a couple of days ahead in my studies. I'll do a couple more tomorrow, but I can help you now."

"Good. How about filing these height and weight figures into each kid's folder?"

She took one, found the folder, and dropped the small paper into it. "Could I talk to you first, Mr.

Brickner?" she asked. "It's important."

"Sure." He left the room a moment, returning with two cans of ginger ale. Handing one to her, he motioned to a chair. "OK, Shelby, shoot."

She calmly told him all that she'd overheard. When she finished, she sat quietly, waiting for his reply.

"Do you know the boy?" he finally asked.

"No, but I've seen him around."

He sat quietly as they drank their sodas. When he finished, he set his can on the corner of his desk. "I'll get a list of the kids in that study hall," he said. "Now, would you like to finish sticking these slips into the files?"

"Sure."

He walked from the room, and she stuck over two hundred small slips of paper into the correct files. Then, after looking around for something else to do, she approached the principal's secretary. "I'm not very good at finding things to do," she said. "Could I help you until Mr. Brickner gets back?"

She'd just started running off an announcement on the copy machine when the principal returned. "Go on back with him," the secretary said. "I can handle this."

"Miss Hilton knew the boy right off," Mr. Brickner said. "She'd noticed the conversation and planned to talk to me about it." He turned and smiled at Shelby. "It looks as if your suspicions were correct," he said. "I'm going to call both boys in right now. Think you can handle it?"

"You mean, can I keep my mouth shut? I think I can. I had a tough time in study hall, but I did. I'll keep quiet. I can't wait to get my flute back!"

In a few minutes, the two boys entered the office.

"Sit down, boys," the principal said. When they did as he asked, he went on. "I understand you have a flute for sale, Jon," Mr. Brickner said.

Jon's face turned white. He shook his head. "The guys were just kidding around."

"You said you did," the other boy said. "I thought you really did."

Mr. Brickner stood up behind his desk. "Look here, Jonathan Greenflower, *I'm* not kidding around. Where did you get this flute you're trying to sell?"

Shelby saw sweat drops appear on Jon's upper lip. His head dropped. "I said I don't have a flute."

Mr. Brickner reached for the phone. "I'll just get your parents, Jon. It'll take only a minute."

He punched down three numbers before Jon yelled, "Don't do that, Mr. Brickner." Then he put his face in his hands, and his shoulders started shaking.

Mr. Brickner put down the phone and leaned on his elbows. He waited a few moments for Jon to settle down. Then he cleared his throat. Jon still shook. "We have to continue this conversation, Jon," he said quietly. "Can you sit up and listen?"

Jon gave his eyes a swipe with both hands. He pulled his shoulders back. Then his eyes met the principal's. "I'm all right."

"Good. Why did you take Shelby's flute, Jon?"

"Because . . ." a big sigh escaped his lips ". . . she's so perfect. No matter what I say to her, she's always nice. I just wanted to see what she'd do." He smiled then and shook his head. "Boy, I saw, didn't I? She had a cow over that silly flute."

"You were about to sell it?"

He shook his head vigorously. "No way. I was just kidding the guys. I was going to give it back. Then it sort of got out of hand when she broke my foot. I didn't want to tell my folks who did it, but they forced me."

Mr. Brickner picked up a pencil and examined the point. "They're going to have to hear the rest, you know." He brightened and turned to Shelby. "You two can go now if you like. It's about time for the last bell."

"Will you get my flute for me?" Shelby asked.

"I'll give it to you first thing in the morning," Jon said. "I'm sorry, Shelby. I just did it to rile you." He grinned again. "I never saw anything work so well in my life."

Shelby hurried to meet the bus.

"You'll never guess," she told Molly when they got off. "Jon did take my flute."

"You already knew that. Looks as if your life's back to its usual wonderful way. Now why don't you fix mine up so it's as great?"

Shelby looked at Molly. "I'm sorry, Molly. Are things worse than usual?"

Molly shook her head. "Just the usual rotten stuff." They reached the driveways, and Molly turned to leave. "It's OK, Shelby. Some people are just born to have all the luck."

"You know what?" Shelby said. "Losing my mom was about the worst thing that could happen to anyone. But the Bible says God will change our tears of sadness to tears of joy. And that's what He's done for me, Molly. I wish you loved Him the way I do."

Molly hung her head. "I might sometime. But maybe He's just your God, Shelby."

The girls ran in opposite directions, each to her own home.

"Hey, that's great, kiddo," Aunt Rachel said when Shelby told her what had happened at school. "I hope they put him in jail and throw away the key."

"I don't know, Auntie," Shelby said. "I felt sorry for him." She grinned. "And that's going to make it a lot easier to do what I have to do. I have to ask Jon to forgive me. That means I have to get rid of all my bad feelings for him. Then I have to ask God to forgive me. And I'll mean it this time. I'm sure He's really disappointed in me, but He'll be happy when I make things right. As usual, God's right. I should have been good to Jon, even when he was mean to me. Then I wouldn't have all this asking-to-be-forgiven stuff to do.

"Know what else, Auntie? Molly just told me I'm one of the lucky kids, and you know what? I agree with her. I'm lucky to have you, Uncle, Sandy, and of course, my little Bunky. Molly's right. I wish she could be as lucky."